I0635918

Savage Angels MC Series Book Twelve

Kathleen Kelly

Savage Angels

Savage Angels MC Series Book Twelve

Kathleen Kelly

All efforts have been made to ensure the correct grammar and punctuation in the book. If you do find any errors, please e-mail Kathleen Kelly: kathleenkellyauthor@gmail.com
Thank you.

Disclaimer: The material in this book contains graphic language and sexual content and is intended for mature audiences, ages 18 and older.

ISBN: 978-1-922883-09-4

Edited by Swish Design & Editing
Proofreading by Swish Design & Editing
Book Design by Swish Design & Editing
Cover design by Clarise Tan at CT Cover Creations
Cover Image Copyright
First Edition 2024

DEDICATION

This is for you, dear reader.
Book Twelve in what was supposed to be a five-
book series, sees the end of the
original Savage Angels MC.
Because of you, the Savage Angels evolved
and became a best-selling series.
Thank you from the bottom of my heart.

There will be more in late 2024, with the next
generation spreading their wings.
I hope you enjoy them as well.

SAVAGE
angels

CHAPTER
1

DANE REYNOLDS
President, Savage Angels MC

The roar of my bike echoes through the streets as I roll into Tourmaline, victorious from our mission in Vegas. The sun is setting, casting a fiery orange glow on the asphalt beneath Dirt and me. As we pull up to the Savage Angels MC clubhouse, the rest of the club spills out, cheering and slapping our backs. I can feel their respect for me like a palpable energy, but none of it matters if I can't get in touch with Kat.

"Fuck!" I mutter under my breath, staring at my phone.

No missed calls.

No texts.

Nothing.

"Hey, Prez," Bear shouts over the commotion, "You good?"

"Can't reach Kat." My voice is tight with worry, barely audible over the din.

"Shit." He frowns, understanding my unease.

"Everybody, inside," I bark, waving my hand toward the clubhouse.

The party can wait—priorities first.

"Sorry, brother. Gotta make a call," I say to Dirt as I stalk away, heading for some privacy. "Kat, pick up, darlin'." Ringing. Voicemail. "Goddammit." I redial her number again. "Come on, come on." Another try. Same result. "*Fuck*!" The word shoots out like a bullet, anger and worry mingling in one potent cocktail.

I run my fingers through my long, dark hair, feeling the sweat bead on my forehead. I need to hear her voice to know she is okay.

"Pick up, Kat. Please." Just ringing. Empty air on the other end. "Where the fuck are you?" I whisper, desperation creeping in.

The weight of uncertainty bears down on me, drowning out the laughter and celebration erupting from within the clubhouse.

"Dammit, Kat, answer the phone." I try her number again, pacing my room like a caged animal. Voicemail. "Darlin', it's Dane. Call me back as soon as you can. I need to know you're safe."

I send a string of texts, each more frantic than the last, but nothing comes back. No comforting words, no acknowledgment. Just silence.

"Fuckin' hell," I mutter, slamming my fist against the wall. My knuckles throb, but the pain is nothing compared to the gnawing fear in my gut.

"Dane?" a voice interrupts my turmoil. Judge stands in the doorway, his wiry frame exuding calm. "Salvatore has been trying to call you."

Flicking through my contacts, I dial Salvatore, who answers on the first ring. "Dane?"

"Do you know where Kat and my children are?"

"Tony has them."

Tony is Sal's personal security and was sent to Hawaii to keep an eye on our loved ones.

"What the hell is going on? Where's Kat?"

"Tony didn't want to take any chances. He thought he recognized some of Don Abruzzi's men, so he moved everyone. They're safe." At his words, I sag onto my bed. "He's got them stashed in a safe house. They're fine, Dane, I promise."

"Then why the fuck isn't she answering my calls?" I snap, frustration bubbling to the surface.

"Tony wanted to keep things on the down-low, make sure nobody could track them. He made them ditch their phones. I'm sorry, Dane. I should've called you sooner."

"Damn right, you should've," I growl, trying to steady my breathing. "Get me a secure line to talk to her, Sal. And I mean *now*."

"Of course," he replies, his voice firm and resolute. "I'll try to set it up as soon as possible, but I need Tony to ring me as even I don't know where they are. You're not the only one wanting to hear your wife's or children's voices."

"Sorry, Sal, and thank you." I nod, letting out a heavy sigh.

At least Kat is safe.

That's something.

Ending the call, I fall back on the bed and rub my throbbing temples. My world is spinning out of control, but one thing remains constant—my burning need to protect those I love.

"Whatever it takes," I vow to myself, my determination hardening. "No matter the cost."

Dammit! I can't shake the nagging feeling that something is off.

My gut churns with worry as I pace the clubhouse, my boots thudding heavily against the worn wooden floor. Kat's silence gnaws at me, eating away my resolve like a persistent parasite.

"Fuck this," I mutter, pulling out my phone again.

No new messages, no missed calls—nothing. My frustration peaks, and I slam my fist into the nearest wall, the sharp pain momentarily distracting me from the relentless uncertainty.

"Prez, you all right?" Dirt appears in the doorway, his face creased with concern. He stands tall despite the ache in his shoulder. His loyalty to the club is unwavering, even in the face of his pain.

"Still can't get a hold of Kat," I spit, shoving my phone back into my pocket. "Somethin' ain't right."

"Maybe she's just busy, Dane," suggests Jonas, trying to ease my mind.

But I know better. Kat always makes time for our calls, no matter how hectic her schedule gets.

"Judge, Bear, Jonas, get your asses in here," I bark as I stalk into the chapel, our meeting room, with Dirt following close behind.

I'm unwilling to waste any more time. The men hurry in, their expressions a mix of attentiveness and apprehension.

"Prez?" Judge asks, his wiry frame is tense and ready for action.

"Have you heard from Jasmin?" Judge shakes his head. "Find out anything you can about their whereabouts. I don't care if you have to scour the goddamn island. We need eyes on her," I order, my voice steely with resolve. "I mean *all of them.*"

"Already on it, Prez," Bear replies, his newly slimmed-down figure betraying none of the exhaustion I know he must feel. "I've got contacts working on the ground in Hawaii. They'll keep us in the loop."

"Good." I nod, trying to rein in my growing unease. "I *need* to know she's safe."

"Hey," Jonas lays a reassuring hand on my shoulder. "We'll find her and the others. We're all worried."

"Thanks, brother," I murmur, clapping him on the back before turning away.

My heart races with fear and anticipation as if preparing for an unknown battle.

My brothers disperse to carry out their tasks while I focus on quelling the rising tide of panic within me. Kat is the rock that holds me steady in turbulent waters. Without her, I feel adrift in a storm I can't see or understand. But I'll be damned if I let anything happen to her or the kids.

"Come hell or high water," I whisper, my voice barely audible in the now-empty room. "I'll keep you safe, Kat. Always." And with that promise hanging heavy in the air, I begin the agonizing wait for news.

My boots tap out a staccato rhythm on the chapel floor, a relentless march echoing my mounting frustration. I can't shake the feeling something is off, that Kat and the kids are in danger. It gnaws at me.

"Fuck this." I halt my pacing as a decision takes root in my mind.

Salvatore isn't taking my calls, and Kat or my sister, Emily, haven't called me back. If no one can find them, then I'll go to Hawaii myself and tear the whole goddamn island apart until I have them safe in my arms.

"Prez?" Dirt's voice cracks through my thoughts. "Any news?"

"Nothing yet," I growl, slamming my fist onto the desk. "But I can't just sit here waiting for shit to happen. I'm going to Hawaii."

"Are you sure?" Dirt asks, concern lacing his words. "Sal says they're okay at a safe house, and we've got our guys searching all over the island. They'll find her, Dane."

"I know," I concede, rubbing my forehead. "But I'd feel better if I heard her voice and… I need to be there. I can't do fuck-all from here."

"All right, Prez." Dirt sighs. "I'll get everything ready for you. Just say the word."

"Thanks, brother."

The thought of finding Kat myself lights a fire in my gut, pushing me to act.

"Before you go…" Judge walks toward us. "We got wind of something. Might not be much, but there's been chatter about some new players trying to move into our territory. Could be connected to what's happening with Kat."

"Keep an eye on it," I order, my jaw clenched. "Find out who they are and what they want. I need to know everything."

"Roger that, Prez," Judge replies.

"Kat," I whisper, staring out at the dark sky. "Hang on, baby. I'm coming." And with that, my mind is made up. No matter what it takes, no matter how many miles separate us, I will find her.

The sun is on the horizon, casting an ominous orange glow over the near-empty streets of Tourmaline this morning. My heart pounds in my chest, each beat echoing my frustration and fear. I can't shake the nagging feeling that something is wrong, that Kat is slipping further from my grasp.

"Fuck!" I growl, slamming my fist onto the worn wooden table in the chapel. The pain barely registers as my thoughts race, searching for any clue as to where she could be. My gut churns with the need to find, protect, and make sure she is safe.

Just as I am about to lose it completely, my phone buzzes on the table, the screen lighting up with 'UNKNOWN.' Snatching it up, I answered with a forceful, "Hello?"

"Dane," Tony's voice comes through, laced with exhaustion. "I got 'em. Kat, Emily, and the kids. They're safe."

"Jesus Christ." I exhale, the relief flooding through me like a tidal wave. I lean back against the chair, suddenly weak in the knees. "Where are they?"

"Safe house in Hawaii," he explains quickly, sensing my urgency. "Had to keep 'em out of sight, away from prying eyes. It's been tough getting a secure line, but they're okay. I promise."

"Thank fuck," I mutter, running a hand through my hair. But as the relief begins to ebb, frustration takes its place. "Why the hell didn't you tell me sooner? You know how worried I've been? Put my wife on the phone *now*."

"Sorry, Dane, I really am," Tony replies sincerely. "But it had to be done. I couldn't risk anyone finding out their location. You know how it is. And Salvatore... he wanted me to handle things on this end."

Salvatore—the name carries weight, but my priority is Kat and my children. I grit my teeth, reining in my anger.

"All right," I say, trying to keep my voice steady. "But from now on, I need to be kept in the loop. You hear me? I can't protect them if I don't know what's going on."

"Understood. It won't happen again," Tony promises. "I can't put her on the phone... she's not with me."

"What the fuck?"

"She's at the safe house. I couldn't risk her or the others until I know it's safe. Not only do I have to look out for possible threats, but with her and The Grinders being famous, it's hard to keep them out of the public eye. The last thing we need is a fan or the paparazzi alerting the world to their whereabouts. If it makes you feel better, she's as frustrated as you are. Kat sure has a temper, but she understands I'm trying to keep everyone safe."

"Good," I reply, my mind racing with a million questions and concerns. But for now, knowing they are safe will have to be enough. It's what matters most. "Just... take care of 'em, Tony. They mean everything to me. Can't you buy a burner phone?"

"It's what I'm calling you on, and I've just purchased six more." Tony pauses, then says, "I'll guard them with my life."

"Thanks, Tony. I know. I'm frustrated because I'm not there." I sigh. "How is everyone holding up?"

Tony chuckles. "They're all busy talking about another album. Kat is occupied with music, and

Emily is feeding everyone, but if they have any downtime, both women make my job almost impossible."

"That's my girl." I laugh as some of the uncertainty leaves me. "What are you doing to keep the kids calm?"

"There's a pool and a private beach. So far, they're okay."

"Tell them I love them."

"Will do." Tony ends the call.

Taking a deep breath, I force myself to focus. I can't let my frustration cloud my judgment. For the club and my family, I need to stay sharp. They depend on me, and I won't let them down. From now on, I'll be even more vigilant about staying in touch with Kat and the kids, no matter the distance.

"All right," I say out loud to myself, clenching my fists as I make up my mind. "Time to get shit done."

The next morning, I gather Dirt, Jonas, Judge, and Bear in the clubhouse. Their loyalty to the club and respect for me has never wavered, and I need that kind of unwavering support now more than ever.

"Listen up, boys," I start, ensuring they all know

how serious this situation is. "I need to make sure we can always reach each other, especially my family. We're going to strengthen our communication channels so we can stay connected. No more delays, no more being left in the dark. Got it?"

"Got it, Prez," Dirt replies, his gruff voice echoing my resolve.

"Good." I nod, looking into the eyes of each of my brothers. "Jonas, I want you to work on setting up encrypted lines between us and the safe house. Make sure it's secure and untraceable."

"Can do, Prez," Jonas says firmly. "Before all this, Guru was already making plans."

Guru is our resident hacker and computer wizard.

"Judge, Bear, I need you two to devise a contingency plan just in case things go south. If we have to move them again, we need to be ready."

"Understood, Prez," Judge says while Bear nods in agreement.

"All right then," I say, satisfied with the direction we are heading. "Let's get to work. And remember, we do this for our family and the club. We're all in this together."

"Always, Prez," Dirt adds, a determined look in his eyes.

The others nod in agreement. I may not be able to talk to Kat at the moment, but I can make damn sure nothing like this ever happens again. With our communication channels improving, I know protecting my family and club will be a lot easier. We will face any threat that comes our way, and no matter what it takes, I know with my brothers by my side, we will conquer anything and everything in our path.

CHAPTER
2

SALVATORE AGOSTINO
Captain, Abruzzi Crime Family

I'm being driven up the fucking wall, having not heard from Emily in hours. I know she's safe with Tony, but being unable to talk to her is like a knife twisting in my gut. The silence in this house is suffocating, and all I want is to hear her voice reassuring me everything will be okay. But I can't have that, not right now.

"Dammit," I say to myself as I pace back and forth in my office, the worn wooden floorboards creaking beneath my shoes. My fists are clenched so tight my knuckles turn white, and I feel like my skull is about to crack open from all the worry and frustration bottled up inside me.

The air in the room feels heavy like the walls are

closing in.

"Fuck!" I shout, slamming my fist against my desk, sending papers and pens flying everywhere.

It does nothing to quell the storm raging inside me, though—if anything, it makes it worse. I force myself to take deep breaths and count to ten. It's a trick Emily taught me when we first got together, something to help keep the anger at bay. And right now, I need all the help I can get to stay focused.

The only thing giving me a little solace is the knowledge Tony is with her. He would stand between her and the devil himself to keep them all safe. Tony may be getting older, but he's still sharper than men half his age. Him moving them all to a safer place proves this.

For now, though, all I can do is pace, wait, and pray they're secure. And when the time comes, I'll be ready to strike with a vengeance that will make the earth shake and the heavens tremble.

Just hold on a little bit longer, amare.

I'm coming for you.

"Let's go, Lorenzo," I growl as I storm out of my house.

My right-hand man falls in step beside me as we make our way to the car. The drive to Don Abruzzi's place feels like an eternity, but we finally pull into the driveway to his extravagant mansion.

"Remember, play it cool," Lorenzo warns as we enter the opulent estate.

He knows me too well—knows I'm wound tight with worry over my family, and one wrong word could send me over the edge.

I take a deep breath, trying to keep my emotions in check.

One of the Don's henchmen opens the door.

"Sal. The Don will be with you in a moment." He opens the door wider. "You know the way to his office?"

"You know I fucking do."

The man's eyes widen, but he says nothing as we stride through the Don's home and enter his office. I throw open the door, and when Lorenzo and I are inside, I slam it shut, the noise echoing through the house. My anger is like a volcano as they make us wait for Don Abruzzi. This shit's an insult to me and my standing within our family.

"Son of a bitch," I grumble under my breath, pacing around the room with clenched fists. "Can't even show his face on time."

My eyes flick to the expensive paintings hanging on the walls and the crystal glasses next to bottles filled with top-shelf liquor. Every detail of this room screams power and control, and it only fuels my rage.

"Salvatore, calm down," Lorenzo reminds me.

But I can't. Not when so much is at stake. Not when every fiber of my being tells me something's not right about this whole situation.

The door swings open, and I say, "Finally."

Don Abruzzi saunters into the room, wearing a self-satisfied smirk that makes me want to wipe it off his smug face.

"Salvatore, my apologies for the delay," he states as if he hasn't made us wait like pawns in his twisted game. "What brings you here?"

"Cut the bullshit, Don," I snap, my voice laced with barely contained fury. "You know damn well why I'm here. Las Vegas... my territory. I've got word your men have been encroaching on it, making moves they have no right to make."

"Is that so?" Don Abruzzi feigns surprise, his dark eyes narrowing. "And you're sure it's my men?"

"Who else would it be?" I shoot back, my anger boiling over. "You think I don't know what you're up to? You think I can't see through your little schemes?"

"Careful, Salvatore," he warns, his voice dripping with menace. "Accusations like that can be dangerous."

"Fuck your threats, Don," I growl, stepping closer

and forcing myself to look him in the eye. "I want answers. *Now.*"

"All right, all right," he concedes, holding up his hands in mock surrender. "There may have been some... misunderstandings regarding our operations in Las Vegas. But I assure you, it won't happen again."

"See that it doesn't," I say coldly.

My mind races with thoughts of what I'll do if I find out he's lying or discover he's still trying to undermine me and my territory.

"Of course, Salvatore," Don Abruzzi replies smoothly. "After all, we are family, aren't we?"

"Family," I spit out, the word leaving a bitter taste in my mouth. "Just remember, Don... family doesn't betray each other, and if I find out otherwise..." I let the threat hang in the air, the unspoken promise clear as day.

Don Abruzzi sits then leans back in his chair, a smug grin plastered on his face as he casually remarks, "You know, Salvatore, it's interesting you should bring up Las Vegas because I've heard some rather unsettling news about the Savage Angels lately."

"Unsettling how?" I demand, my eyes narrowing suspiciously.

"Disappearances. Killings." He lets the words hang in the air. "Seems your little motorcycle club friends are dropping like flies out there."

"What are you talking about?" My voice comes out low and dangerous, but Don Abruzzi chuckles, clearly enjoying my discomfort.

"Come now, Salvatore. Surely, you didn't think I'd leave you completely unscathed after our last encounter?" His smile widens, revealing teeth that gleam like daggers. "You're not the only one with power in this city, my friend."

My face grows hot, rage boiling beneath the surface as I stare him down. "You bastard," I seethe. "You had something to do with them disappearing?"

"Of course," he replies, his tone nonchalant. "You didn't really think I'd let you undermine me with no consequences, did you?"

"How did I undermine you? I pay you a gratuity every month, and those men were innocent," I snarl, every muscle in my body tensing as I fight the urge to lunge at him right here and now. "Tell me what happened to the Savage Angels members, Don. And tell me now."

"Your *gratuity* is an insult. What are you going to do, Salvatore? You're in *my* house, surrounded by *my* men. Do you really think you can hurt me?" he taunts.

"Watch me," I growl, meeting his eyes with a steely glare. "You may have your men here, but don't think for a second you can hide behind them forever. I'll find the truth eventually, and when I do, there will be hell to pay."

"Such big words for a man so out of his depth," Don Abruzzi sneers, but I can see the flicker of uncertainty in his eyes. He knows I'm not bluffing, and it scares him.

"Start talking, Don," I say, my voice barely more than a whisper. "Tell me everything you know about those killings, and maybe, just maybe, we can come to some sort of understanding."

"Maybe," he echoes, the ghost of a smile playing on his lips. "But then again, maybe not."

Don Abruzzi rocks back in his chair, a sly grin spreading across his face as he watches my rage boil over.

"All right, Salvatore," he drawls, finally deciding to spill the truth. "I'll admit it. I ordered the hit on those Savage Angels bastards."

His voice oozes arrogance, and I can hear the sadistic pleasure lacing every word. The bastard is really enjoying this—the thought of taking control of the casinos and snuffing out lives to get what he wants.

"Those casinos should have been mine from the start. So, I had to eliminate the competition, you see." Don Abruzzi's eyes gleam with malice.

My fists clench at my sides, knuckles white from the force of my grip. My teeth grind together, the sound echoing in my head like nails on a chalkboard as I fight to contain the anger threatening to consume me.

"Is this a game to you?" I spit out, my voice dangerously low.

"Ah, Salvatore," he says with a dark chuckle. "Business is always a game, and I play to win."

My mind races—thoughts of revenge and retribution for the fallen fill every corner of my consciousness. I won't let him get away with this. I can't. The Savage Angels and my men he killed deserve justice, and I'm going to be the one to deliver it.

"Enjoy your victory lap while it lasts, Don," I say through gritted teeth. "Because I promise you, there will be consequences for your actions."

"Bold words," he replies, his smile never leaving his face. "But remember this, Salvatore... bold words often come back to haunt those who speak them."

"Consider me haunted," I snarl, turning on my heel and storming out of the room.

The fight has only just begun, and I don't intend to lose.

With the memory of Don Abruzzi's twisted smile

and chilling confession still branded in my mind, I storm back to my office, my blood boiling. My fists remain clenched and my knuckles white as if I'm ready to tear him apart with my bare hands. But I know that won't be enough—not for me and not for the Savage Angels.

"Justice," I growl, my voice shaking with fury. "I swear on everything I hold dear, there will be justice for those who were taken from us."

"Sal, we're with you," Lorenzo says, his eyes showing unwavering support.

The rest of my men nod in agreement, their loyalty unwavering. It strengthens my resolve and hardens my heart against any doubt or fear that may try to creep in.

My gaze locks onto the framed photo of my family on my desk, reminding me of what's at stake. Emily, my beautiful wife, and our children—their lives depend on me ending this madness.

"Listen up," I say, my voice low and dangerous but steady. "We're going to bring down Don Abruzzi and every last one of those snake bastards in his operation who oppose us. They'll pay for what they've done, and I'll make damn sure they never forget it."

"Damn right," Lorenzo agrees, fire in his eyes. "They messed with the wrong crew."

"First things first," I declare, steeling myself for the battle ahead. "We need to gather intel on all the

Abruzzi Crime Family's operations. Find their weaknesses and exploit them. We hit them where it hurts, and we don't stop until they're begging for mercy."

As they file out of the office, I take a moment to collect myself. The weight of the situation settles on my shoulders, but I don't let it break me. Instead, I use it as fuel, a fire that burns inside me, pushing me forward.

In the deafening silence of my office, a plan begins to form in the back of my mind—a plan that will bring down Don Abruzzi and restore balance to our world. No matter how long it takes, no matter what it costs me, I won't rest until I see it through for the Savage Angels, my family, and every life destroyed by the Abruzzi Crime Family's greed and cruelty.

When my emotions are in check, I sit behind my desk, pour myself a glass of red wine, and dial Dane. He needs to be updated on Don Abruzzi and what he's done.

"Sal?" Dane's voice comes through the line, strong and steady as always.

"Dane, you aren't going to fucking believe this," I snarl, struggling to keep my rage in check. "That son of a bitch, Don Abruzzi, was behind it all. The motherfucker ordered the hits on my men and the Savage Angels."

"Jesus Christ," Dane growls, his fury apparent even through the phone. "What are we going to do about it?"

"We're going to bring the bastard down, Dane," I reply, conviction hardening my voice. "We're going to hit him where it hurts, and we won't stop until he's begging for mercy. This is war, brother."

"Count me in, Sal," Dane says without hesitation. "The Savage Angels have your back. We'll take those fuckers down together."

"Thanks, man," I say, my gratitude genuine. "First, we need intel. I want everything on the Abruzzis' operations, his allies, and his weak spots. We have to know what we're up against."

"Already on it," Dane assures me. "I have some contacts who can dig up everything we need to know. Give me a couple of days, and we'll have the info."

"Good," I reply, already envisioning our next move. "Once we have that, we'll plan our first strike. This ends now, Dane. No more of our brothers fall because of that piece of shit."

"Agreed," Dane says firmly. "We're in this together, Sal. We'll make damn sure Abruzzi pays for what he's done."

"Damn right," I affirm, my resolve unwavering.

As I hang up the phone, I know dark times lie ahead. There will be bloodshed and heartache, but it's a price I'm willing to pay for justice and vengeance.

This is war, and we *will* emerge victorious.

CHAPTER 3

SALVATORE

While leaning against the cold brick wall, the stench of gasoline and sweat mingle with the bitter taste of betrayal in my mouth. Don Abruzzi's words echo in my head like a bad tune, and his smug grin burns behind my eyelids. The thought of the Savage Angels members disappearing unsettles me, and it doesn't add up. I know deep down, trusting the Abruzzi Crime Family is like playing Russian roulette with a fully loaded gun, but I worked my way up through their ranks, and I thought I'd found myself a place there.

"Fuck," I mutter, running a hand through my hair.

My thoughts are a goddamn storm, swirling and churning like a tempest inside me. I need to talk to

Dane. We must figure this shit out before everything we've built crumbles to dust.

Pushing myself away from the wall, I stalk through the alley, my boots crunching on broken glass and discarded cigarette butts as I make my way toward the Savage Angels clubhouse in Chicago. The neon sign flickers above the entrance, casting eerie shadows over the cracked pavement. I push open the door, the familiar scent of alcohol and leather washing over me.

"Salvatore!" Dane's voice booms across the room when he spots me. He's standing at the bar with a beer in one hand and his sergeant-at-arms, Dirt, standing next to him.

"Hey, Dane." I force a tight smile, swallowing the unease crawling up my throat. "We need to talk. Somewhere private."

His blue eyes narrow, concern flashing across his rugged face. He nods and gestures for me to follow him through a cramped hallway to an office.

"What's going on?" he asks, shutting the door behind us. His towering frame seems to fill the small space, making the walls press in even closer. I can't shake the feeling of being trapped like rats in a cage.

"We know the Don ordered the hits on our men. I think he did it to stick it to me for getting into business with you in the first place."

"We've always known he was an ambitious prick."

"He's a threat to everything we've built. The Don will tear every business dealing we've ever made together to prove *he* knows best."

"What do we do?"

"First, we have to find the missing men, then we need to expose Don Abruzzi for the snake he is and take him down before he becomes more powerful."

"Sounds like a plan," Dane replies, a grim smile on his lips. "Let's get to work."

The smell of gasoline and burned rubber fills my nostrils as I pace the garage, unable to shake the heavy feeling in my chest. Dane stands nearby, talking to the president of the Chicago chapter, Onyx, in hushed voices. The man is a fucking machine, always ready to throw down for his club and those he loves.

"Sal," he says, motioning for me to come closer. "I need you to understand something here. The Savage Angels are loyal to the bone. We don't break or bend, and we sure as hell don't betray our own. You can trust us to have your back."

Onyx nods. "Dane is right. We can't let Don Abruzzi get away with killing our members. I've had three men go missing. I assumed they'd moved on, but now I assume they've been put down."

I look into Dane's ice-blue eyes, searching for any sign of doubt or hesitation. "You'd go against the Abruzzi Crime Family? For me and mine?"

"Damn straight," Dane replies without missing a beat. "We're family, Sal. When one of us is threatened, we all stand together."

"And it's not just you and yours. It's not the first time the Abruzzis have overstepped," Onyx says as he crosses his arms across his chest.

"Even if it gets bloody?" I ask, knowing full well that this fight won't end without casualties on both sides.

"Especially if it gets bloody. You know what they say... blood makes the grass grow."

I let out a humorless chuckle as does Onyx. Going against Don Abruzzi is like poking a sleeping lion with a stick—sooner or later, the damn thing is going to wake up and tear you apart. But what choice do we have?

"All right, but we need to be smart about this. The Abruzzi Crime Family has deep pockets and powerful friends. If we're going to take them on, we need allies of our own."

"Agreed." Dane nods thoughtfully. "There are other families out there who've been just as fucked over by Don Abruzzi's greed and ambition. You need to reach out to them, make them see we're all in this together."

"Strength in numbers," I muse, my mind already racing with possibilities.

But as much as I want to believe we could pull this off, there is one nagging thought I can't shake.

"Listen, Dane, I'm not going to lie... I'm worried for my family and yours. If we do this, if we go against Don Abruzzi and his crew, there's a good chance the shitstorm isn't going to end at our doorstep. It's going to come for our wives, our kids... every-fucking-one we care about."

"Sal," Dane replies, his expression deadly serious, "This is war, and in war, people get hurt. But if we don't stand up now, and we continue to allow Abruzzi to keep running roughshod over us, we're just as good as dead, anyway. Besides..." he adds, clapping me on the shoulder, "... we've faced down worse threats than some two-bit crime boss, haven't we?"

"We haven't seen anything like the war that's coming."

Onyx drags a shoulder up to his ear. "The Abruzzis haven't seen anything like a war with the Savage Angels. We outnumber them. Yes, we will lose men, but there's no reason to think we won't come out on top."

"Exactly," Dane says, a wicked grin spreading

across his face. "Now, let's get to work and show these scumbags who they're messing with."

My heart is pounding like a jackhammer, our decision weighing heavy on my soul. As much as I believe in Dane and our cause, I can't help but think about the backlash Don Abruzzi will rain down on us.

"Sal," Dane says, snapping me out of my thoughts. "You have to focus. We need to act fast if we're going to stand a chance."

"All right," I reply, taking a deep breath. "Let's hear your plan, Dane."

"We can't just go in guns blazing. We need allies... people who aren't afraid to stand up to Abruzzi and his goons. Other crime families." He takes a breath before continuing, "Plenty of them have a beef with Abruzzi. If we can get them on our side, it'll give us the numbers within your organization to take him down."

"Okay," I say, rubbing my chin. "Makes sense. But how do we convince them to join us?"

"Easy." Dane grins. "We show them what they have to gain. If we can promise them a piece of

Abruzzi's territory, they'll jump at the chance to help us."

"Sounds risky." The thought of going against Abruzzi still gnaws at me. "What if they turn on us once they get what they want?"

"Then we'll deal with them when the time comes," Dane says firmly. "But right now, we need all the help we can get."

I sigh, knowing he is right. As much as I hate the idea of making deals with other members of the Abruzzi Crime Family, it is our best shot at fighting back against Don Abruzzi and protecting our families.

"All right, let's do this."

"Good." Dane nods, slapping me on the shoulder. "Now, let's get to work and show these bastards who they're really fucking with."

My thoughts race in a million different directions. My wife and children's safety weighs heavily on my mind, and the thought of taking on the Abruzzi Crime Family sends chills down my spine. The danger is real, but so is the need to protect our loved ones.

Dane is watching me, his blue eyes waiting for an answer.

"Listen, Dane, I get what you're saying, but we can't just go up against Abruzzi without seriously thinking about consequences. If we fail, he'll come after us, our families... it'll be a bloodbath."

Savage Angels

Dane crosses his arms over his broad chest, his expression serious yet understanding. "I know it isn't easy, Sal, but we have to do what's right, not just what's easy. We have honor and loyalty to uphold. That means putting the well-being of our families and club before any allegiance to that snake, Don Abruzzi."

His words hit me like a freight train. Part of me knows he is right, but the other part can't shake the fear that grips my heart. My wife, Emily, and our kids—they are my world. What kind of man would I be if I didn't do everything in my power to keep them safe?

"Right." I sigh, meeting Dane's gaze. "But if we do this, we have to make damn sure we have all our bases covered. No loose ends."

"Agreed," Dane replies, his voice steady as ever. "We'll gather our allies, strengthen our position, and ensure everyone involved knows what's at stake. We'll face whatever comes our way as a team."

"Yeah," I mutter.

"Remember, Sal," Dane says, touching my shoulder. "Love and loyalty above all else."

"Yeah," I whisper, finally accepting the path we are about to take. "Love and loyalty."

The cold wind bites at my face as Dane and I stand outside the clubhouse, our breaths visible in the night air.

"First things first," Dane says, his voice low and serious. "We're going to need to gather some allies."

"I know a few guys who might be willing to lend a hand, but it won't be easy."

"We'll take whatever support we can get. Don Abruzzi has strong links with many law enforcement agencies. We need eyes and ears to alert us if law enforcement will strike at us too."

With an exasperated sigh, I look up at the night sky. "I have my ear to the ground. So far, the Don, to my knowledge, hasn't called in any favors, but he will."

He grins. "Let's make some calls and see who we can trust. The Don isn't the only one with law enforcement on the payroll. Time's running out, and we have to be prepared."

As we walk back inside the clubhouse, I can't shake the weight of my decision from my mind. Standing against Don Abruzzi means risking everything—my loved ones, my position, even my life. But what choice do I have? It is either bow down to the snake or fight for what I believe in.

"Emily and the kids..."

Dane puts his hand on my shoulder, giving it a reassuring squeeze. "I know it isn't easy, Sal. But remember, we're doing this for them, to keep our families safe. Tony is doing a great job keeping them hidden, and we've both sent more men to guard them. We have to trust everyone will do their part and protect them."

Taking a deep breath, I say, "I won't back down... not now, not ever... for those dear to me and everyone I care about."

"Good man," Dane replies, leading me back into the heart of the clubhouse. "We've got a war to win."

The room is thick with tension, the sharp scent of expensive cigars cutting through the musty air. I can feel the weight of their gazes on me. This is it— the sit-down with the Santoro, Bianchi, and Fontana crime families. I've been to enough of these meetings to know everything can change in the blink of an eye.

"Appreciate you all coming," I say, getting

straight to the point. "We have a problem we need to address... Don Abruzzi."

"Whaddya wanna do about 'im?" asks Miro Santoro, his voice gruff and deep.

"Take a stand against him," I reply. "He's gone too far, and it's time someone put him in his place."

"Ya sure ya wanna go down this road?" Dante Fontana chimes in, his brow furrowed. "Goin' against the Don ain't exactly a walk in the park."

"Damn right, it isn't," I admit, my stomach twisting with anxiety. "But there's more at stake here than just our organizations. Our families... our loved ones are all in danger if we don't do something. And I won't stand by while he sinks his fangs into everything we've built."

"All right, Salvatore," says Nino Bianchi, his eyes narrowing as he studies me. "Say we join forces with ya to oppose the Don. Who's gonna lead the charge? Who's gonna rule our families?"

"Let's not worry about that just yet," I reply, trying to keep my voice steady. "We need to focus on building our alliance and getting our people ready for what's coming. We'll figure out the rest once we've secured our position."

"Is this really the best option?" Dante Fontana questions me again, his skepticism palpable.

"Look..." I sigh, rubbing my temples as I try to find the right words. "I know this isn't an easy decision, but we can't afford to sit back and let Don

Abruzzi destroy everything we've fought for... our families, our businesses, and our way of life. And if we don't stand together now, who knows what he'll do next?"

"Salvatore," Nino Bianchi interjects, a sly smile spreading across his face. "We've been wanting to put that bastard in his place for a long time. So, you got my support."

"Count me in," Miro Santoro grunts, nodding at Dante Fontana, who finally relents with a sigh.

"Together, we'll send Don Abruzzi a message he won't forget. And we'll protect our families, no matter the cost."

"Agreed," they all say in unison, with newfound sense of purpose burning in their eyes.

Deep down, I know I can't avoid the question of who'd rule our families. I have to be strategic, play my cards right, and prove I am worthy of leading this rebellion.

"Time's running out." I steal a glance at my new allies. "And we've got to be ready for whatever is coming our way."

The smoky haze in the dimly lit room clings to every surface, a tangible reminder of the tension that fills the air. The Santoro, Bianchi, and Fontana bosses are watching me like hawks, waiting for me to make my move. I can feel my pulse racing, but I know I can't back down now.

"Right," I say, pushing back from the table and

rising. "We're all in this together and need someone to lead us. I'm thinking that someone should be me."

Their eyes narrow, taking in my words as they gauge my sincerity and strength. It isn't just about opposing Don Abruzzi—it is about making sure our families survive the fallout.

"You know," I continue, my voice steady despite the tremor in my hands. "We aren't alone in this fight. I've been talking with Dane, the leader of the Savage Angels. They're honorable, loyal, and have our backs. We need to bring them into our fold, solidifying our alliance and creating a united front against the Don."

"Salvatore," Miro Santoro speaks up, his voice gravelly and thick with suspicion. "You're askin' us to trust a bunch of bikers. How do we know they won't turn on us?"

I meet his gaze head-on, letting him see the conviction in my eyes. "Dane's my brother-in-law," I reply, never breaking eye contact. "He's like blood to me. And in our world, family is everything. If you can't trust you're own, who can you trust?"

A murmur spreads through the room, and I can see them weighing their options. Their loyalty to me is far from guaranteed, but they know I am their best shot at taking down Don Abruzzi and protecting our interests.

"We'll back you, Salvatore. And we'll work with

the Savage Angels. But you better make sure they stay in line." Lorenzo Bianchi taps the table.

"Of course." I nod, feeling relief wash over me like a tidal wave. "I give you my word the Savage Angels will fight for us and with us. Together, we'll show Don Abruzzi and his cronies what it means to cross us."

As I sit back down, I know the road ahead will be long and bloody, but with my new allies by my side and the Savage Angels watching our backs, we have a fighting chance.

And in this world, sometimes that's all you can ask for.

CHAPTER 4

DANE

The clubhouse's worn leather and smell of cigarette smoke hit me the moment I step inside. Savage Angels MC banners hang from the walls like battle flags, a firm reminder of who we are and what we stand for. My brothers, Dirt, Jonas, Judge, and Bear, are already here, lounging in chairs, waiting for my arrival.

"Okay, boys," I say, snapping my fingers to get their attention. "We've got serious shit to discuss."

"What do you have for us, Prez?" Dirt asks, leaning forward, his scar catching in the dim light.

He's been ready for action ever since he took that bullet to the shoulder protecting my ass, though he hasn't let on how much it's bothering him.

"You all know Onyx, this chapter's president?" They all nod. "This is his house, and we'll be respectful. He's being more than generous by letting us use his chapel without him in it."

"Yeah, he is. Why isn't he in here with us?" Judge chimes in.

I know he's thinking about Jasmine, his woman, and his son, but he's also got our backs.

"I wanted a moment alone with you before we let him in. Here's how it's going to go," I continue, pointing at each of them as I assign their roles. "Dirt, your expertise with weapons is unmatched. You'll be handling our arsenal, making sure we have everything we need here in Chicago."

"Got it, Dane." Dirt nods.

"Jonas, you're our master negotiator. When we need an ally or two, you're the one who can make it happen. I also need you to run surveillance on the Abruzzi's. We need to know where they are and what they're doing."

"Consider it done," Jonas says, his eyes sharp and focused.

"Judge, you're going to stay behind and keep the compound safe. We can't afford any surprises while we're out there."

"Understood," Judge replies, his jaw clenched with unwavering intent.

"Last but not least, Bear," I say, meeting the eyes of our road captain. "You'll be organizing training for those who need it for our Chicago brothers. They gotta be ready when shit hits the fan."

"Roger that, Dane." Bear nods.

"Listen up," I say, leaning in close and lowering my voice. "We have to stand together as one. Loyalty and unity... that's what this club's about. We don't back down, no matter what. These are hard times, but we'll come out on top if we stick together."

"Damn right, Prez," Dirt says, a fire in his eyes. "Savage Angels till the day we die."

"Fuck yeah," the others echo, pounding their fists on the table.

"Good." I point at the clock on the wall. "Let's get to work. Time's a tickin', boys."

As they disperse, heads full of plans and purpose, I'm left alone with my thoughts—*Kat and the kids hidden away in Hawaii.* God, I wish they were safer. But these men, these brothers, they'd take a bullet for me and mine. And I'd do the same for them. That's family.

Dirt's knuckles turn white as he grips the steering wheel, his eyes locked on the road ahead.

Occasionally, he rubs his shoulder, wincing at the movement.

"Fuck," he says under his breath, shifting in his seat.

"You good?"

"Yeah, Prez. I'm not sure you should be with me on this buy."

"You're injured," I state. "We're going to need all the firepower we can get."

"I know, but if things go sideways, I'm not sure I can protect you."

Chuckling, I declare, "I'm here to protect you, brother."

Dirt glances at me, then fixes his gaze back on the road. "It's not like I haven't dealt with these people before, but you never know."

"Not my first rodeo, Dirt."

He nods, his lips in a hard, thin line as he stares straight ahead.

We are in the warehouse district—not a lot of people and many abandoned buildings. Dirt pulls into one of them, a car flashes its lights, and Dirt navigates toward it.

"Stay sharp, Prez."

He stops the car and puts it in park but leaves the engine running. Dirt opens his door, glances at me, and exits. I open my door, and we walk to the other car. A man gets out and strolls to the front of his van and leans against it.

"Dirt! Good to see you." He cocks his head to the side. "Well, shit, if it ain't Dane Reynolds, Kat Saunders' husband."

"*Great*, he's a fan," I whisper to Dirt.

Dirt shakes his head but continues to walk to the man and extends his arm. "Rocco, it's been a while."

He shakes Dirt's hand but keeps staring at me. "Thought you lot were going straight?"

"We are," I state.

Rocco barks out a laugh and walks around the van, opening the back. "Everything you asked for."

Dirt points at the car. "Money's in the trunk."

"It's not a stolen car, is it?"

"It's clean," I answer.

"Hey, you couldn't get me tickets to The Grinders next show in Chicago, can you?"

Tilting my head to the side, I frown at the man. "You like The Grinders?"

"I have all their albums. Kat's voice when she sang "Heaven"?" He holds a hand to his heart. "Sublime."

"Yeah, yeah, Rocco, we get it. You like their music." Dirt closes the back of the van.

"You wound me, Dirt." Rocco stares at me. "I don't like it... I love it."

"Tell you what, if these are all good quality, clean, and work like they should, I'll get you a backstage pass."

Rocco wraps his arms around himself and grins

at me. "For real?"

"For real."

"Damn, man! You're the best." He looks at his surroundings. "Well, nice doing business with you. We should hustle. You never know who's lurking in these old buildings."

Rocco holds out his hand to me, and we shake, then he jogs to the car we came in.

"Interesting guy," I say.

"Yeah, and you promised him, a gun dealer, a meet and greet with your *wife*."

Shrugging, I walk around to the driver's door. "Yeah, I did. Come on, brother, let's get out of here."

CHAPTER
5

JONAS
VP, Savage Angels MC, Tourmaline Chapter

Clinking glasses and murmurs surround me in this dimly lit bar. I have my cell phone pressed against my ear, and my eyes are focused on the glass of vodka I'm swirling.

"Listen," I say firmly. "We need this alliance. The Savage Angels can't stand alone against what's coming, and neither can you. We've got to stick together if we're going to make it through this shitstorm."

"I don't know..." their words trail off, and I can hear the uncertainty in their voices.

"Trust me," I continue, leaning in closer to the phone. "Together, we're stronger than anything they can throw at us. You know it, and I know it. So, what's it going to be?"

There is a long pause and then a sigh. "Sure," they finally reply. "We'll back you up, but you better not let us down. Got it!"

"Wouldn't dream of it. We're in this together, brother."

Ending the call, I signal the bartender for another drink.

What's the old saying? *The enemy of my enemy is my friend.*

There are several smaller street gangs in Chicago who have a beef with the Abruzzis. Getting all of them to join with us has not been easy. They have to know their chances of survival have just increased tenfold. With solid alliances in place, they are one step closer to victory and getting out from under the boot of the Abruzzis.

"The same?" asks the bartender.

"Yeah."

He pours me another, and I raise it in a silent toast to my brothers. Inwardly, I send out a prayer. 'May we stand together until the end.'

The lights cast long shadows across the Savage

Angels' compound in Chicago. Standing here, my gaze is fixed on the perimeter fence, weighing what needs to be done while my brothers prepare for the battle ahead.

"Jonas?" Judge's voice pulls me out of my thoughts.

I cock an eyebrow at him.

"Is everything okay?" Judge asks.

"You need to make sure this place stays safe while we're gone. We can't let them strike at us and win in one of our compounds. It'll weaken us."

"Understood, VP." Judge nods.

"Good man." I lightly punch him on the shoulder before walking into the clubhouse.

Bear is talking to a group of the Chicago chapter's members. He gives me a chin lift, says something to them I can't hear, and saunters over to me.

"Are they ready for whatever's coming?"

"I'll have them fighting like hellhounds by the time this is over." Bear adjusts his jeans.

"Still losing weight?"

He grins. "Yeah." Bear waves a hand in the air, dismissing the conversation about his weight loss. "Most of the chapter here knows how to handle themselves. They've been at odds with local gangs for a long time. They probably know more about guns and death than most chapters."

"Who are their main competitors?"

"The real question is, who isn't?" He crosses his arms. "There's a lot of gang activity in Chicago. We're lucky we established a chapter here years ago. As far as MCs go, we are the largest, but there are lots of turf wars happening between the street gangs."

"Makes you glad we live in a small town, doesn't it?"

"Sure does." Bear nods emphatically.

As I walk away to prepare for the upcoming conflict, I can't help but think about Addy, my woman, who is waiting for me back in Tourmaline. I hope to God she is safe through all this, and we will come out the other side unscathed.

"Jonas," Bear's voice pulls me back to the present. "Help me talk to the boys and see who needs a gun and what they like to use."

"Sounds like a plan." I try to keep my thoughts of Addy at bay as we gather our crew, readying them for the war that is coming.

"Listen up!" Bear bellows, his voice commanding the attention of every man in the room. "You need to be prepared for what's coming. If you need firepower or want a second piece, come see me or Jonas."

Onyx stands. "Some of you already own a gun, but our brothers from Tourmaline have acquired clean firepower, so get yourselves another piece, whether you think you need it or not." Onyx nods at

Bear and me and sits back down.

Standing back, I watch Bear chat with the other men, asking questions and trying his best to give them answers to their worries. He has always been skilled with people, and it makes him a great road captain. He makes sure everyone is comfortable and enjoying themselves.

Focusing on the task ahead, I pull out my cell phone and look for a quiet corner of the clubhouse. Dane asked me to gather intel on the Abruzzi's and their allies. It's been interesting researching the mob families in Chicago. For all their infighting, they stand united against the street gangs and anyone else who tries to muscle in on their business. The days of Al Capone are long gone, but they still abide by a set of rules. The most interesting one is if you kill the head of a family, you can't assume their title. You will never be their leader.

The MC here has close ties to a local gang called the Shadow Syndicate. They don't refer to themselves as a gang but as a nation. It's their members I'm using to keep tabs on the different mafia members. I told them to contact me if the Abruzzis were on the move or involved in unusual activity. I have no texts or missed calls on my cell phone, so I guess no news is good news.

Onyx joins me and sits opposite. He nods at my phone. "Everything okay?"

"Appears so."

Onyx casts a glance around his clubhouse. "It's not our first time dealing with the mob or a gang who needs to be pulled into line. Chicago's a hard city."

"If you're feeling disrespected—"

Onyx holds up a hand. "Not at all. We are one club. If they go after one of us, they go after all of us, and we will strike back. But when the dust settles, and you all go home, what does my chapter get out of it?"

"What do you want?"

Onyx frowns, leans back in his chair, and says, "We're slowly pulling out of businesses that make us a lot of money."

"Drugs and guns," I state flatly.

"Yeah, we aren't all married to a rock star who earns millions."

Scoffing, I say, "If that's what you think of us, then you don't know us at all. Kat's money is Kat's money. Dane was pulling us away from all that long before she came on the scene."

"Yeah, I know."

Slipping my cell phone away, I say, "So, what do you want?"

"Help. The four biggest industries in Chicago are..." Onyx holds up four fingers and puts them down one at a time as he relays, "... manufacturing, transportation, technology, and healthcare. The

Tourmaline chapter already has a freight business established, and we'd like them to expand into Chicago. My city is key to expansion due to our central location, and when we are successful in overthrowing the Abruzzi's, there will be a vacuum, and I'd like to take advantage of it."

"What are we talking about?"

"We have the trucks and the drivers but not the contracts."

Scrubbing a hand down my face, I say, "Sal isn't going to let you take over distribution in Chicago."

"He will if Dane asks him."

Pursing my lips, I give a quick shake of my head. "Sal might be open to a negotiation, but you're not going to get everything."

Onyx leans in. "We *want* the Abruzzi contracts. No more, no less, and we want to be attached to the freight company that operates out of Tourmaline. It's established, it has a good rep, and it'll help with the plans we have for the future of the club here in Chicago." He stands and walks away.

I'm still sitting in the same position when Dane and Dirt walk through the clubhouse doors. I raise a hand to signal them. Dane settles in a chair nearest to me, and Dirt sits opposite us.

"We have a problem."

Dane cocks his head to the side. "With?"

"Onyx." Dane scans the clubhouse looking for him. "He's not here. He rode out a while ago."

"What's the issue?" asks Dirt.

Sighing, I say, "They want the Abruzzi transportation contracts out of Chicago, and they want to fly under Grinders Transport for distribution."

Dane's lips turn down, and he tilts his head from side to side. "Smart. I'll have to talk to Sal for the first part of his demands, but the second is easy. We need to expand. Chicago is a good choice, but as the mother chapter, we'll get a cut."

"Grinders Transport is yours, not the club's," I state.

"Yeah, it is. But for a while now, I've considered expanding throughout the Savage Angels' network. We could dominate the industry and push out UPS."

"And the mother chapter gets a cut of all of it," I reply.

"Yep." Dane grins.

CHAPTER
6

DANE

Leaning against my bike, I take a deep breath. Now, more than ever, I need them to understand we must change if we want to survive.

"Listen up, brothers," I say, catching their attention as they huddle around me. "I've been thinking about the future of the Savage Angels MC, and it's time we start planning for it."

"What do you have in mind, Dane?" Judge asks, his brow furrowed.

"The Grinders Transport is going to branch out into some of the Savage Angels' chapters." They all go silent. "But only if they are clean."

"Clean?" asks Bear.

"Strip clubs, tattoo parlors, garages, real estate… it's where we should be focusing our efforts," I continue. "This way, we can build something legit for our families and future generations. Grinders Transport is mine, but I'm willing to share but only to those who are willing to step away from drugs and guns."

Judge says, "Grinders Transport is the perfect way to move drugs and guns."

"It's not the way. Not anymore," I say.

"Judge is right. We need to spin it in a language we all understand." Jonas smirks. "Making money without the constant threat of prison or death? Count me in, and most of us will feel the same."

"Fuckin' A," Bear adds, giving me a hearty pat on the shoulder. "You lead, we follow, brother." But Dirt looks uneasy, shifting his weight from one foot to the other. I can see the conflict in his eyes, and I know he has something on his mind.

"Speak up, Dirt," I coax. "We're all in this together, brother. If you have concerns, we need to hear them."

"Ah, fuck." He sighs, dragging a hand through his hair. "It's just... I'm getting older, Dane. Sometimes I wonder how much longer I can keep doing this shit."

"You used to say age isn't anything but a number, man." Bear grins at him. "Besides, we aren't talking about riding into battle. We're talking about building a better future for us and our families."

"I know, I know," Dirt admits. "Just sometimes...

it all feels like too much, y'know?"

"Hey," I give him a firm squeeze on his good shoulder. "We've been through hell and back together. You aren't alone in this, brother. We'll figure it out."

Dirt nods, but I have known him for a long time, and something is not right.

"Are we all on the same page? Ready to face whatever comes our way and build a better future for our club?"

They nod, and Bear raises his fist high. These men are in my inner circle, and if they agree with me, then I know most in the MC will come along for the ride, but there will be some, like Dirt, who don't want to change the old ways.

The Chicago chapter clubhouse is overflowing with Savage Angels MC members—those who are patched in and prospects—no outsiders, no women. This is the moment to strike, to rally them for the battles ahead with the Abruzzis, and, internally, get them to let go of the old ways.

"Brothers, we stand here as one, united under the banner of the Savage Angels. We've faced countless challenges, fought through blood and tears, and always come out stronger. Our enemies may try to break us, but they'll learn it isn't possible." I slam my fist on the table. "Every single one of you is essential to this club. Each of you brings something unique, and together, we're unstoppable. No matter what, we have each other's backs, and that's our greatest strength. So, let's show those bastards what we're made of."

"Fuck yeah!" Jonas roars, followed by the rest of the brothers, their voices thundering like a force of nature.

"Remember," I say as I look around the room. "This isn't just about us… it's about our families, our loved ones, and the future we're building for them. We fight not just for ourselves but for everyone who depends on us."

"Damn right, brother," Judge replies, his voice firm and steady.

"Then, let's get to work," I command. "We've got a lot to do, and time's ticking. Stay sharp, and remember, we are the Savage Angels, and nothing can tear us apart."

"Fuckin' A!" Bear shouts, pumping his fist in the air.

"Tomorrow will be a day to test us all." I watch as they disperse, each heading off to tackle their assigned tasks. I know they will give it their all, and this knowledge fills me with pride.

As for me, well, I have my own part to play—one that will test me like never before. But I am ready, willing, and able to face whatever comes my way.

The clubhouse door slams shut, leaving me alone with my thoughts in the dimly lit hallway. I run a hand through my hair and let out a deep breath, trying to steady the storm raging in my chest.

"Fuck," I mutter under my breath, leaning against the wall for support as the weight of responsibility settles heavily on my shoulders. These men, my brothers, are putting their lives on the line for the club and me, and I can't help but feel grateful for their unwavering loyalty. But that gratitude is tempered by worry for my beautiful wife, Kat, and our kids, who are still in hiding.

Pushing away from the wall, I walk over to the small gym they have set up in the back of the clubhouse. The familiar smell of sweat and grit fills the air, reminding me of all the hours I've spent pushing my body to its limits. If I am going to come out of this fight alive, I need to be at my best, mentally and physically.

Rolling my shoulders to loosen them up, I wrap

my hands in tape. My fists connect with the heavy bag, each strike sending a jolt of energy coursing through my veins. As I fall into the rhythm of the workout, my thoughts drift back to Kat—her green eyes that sparkle with defiance and her light brown hair streaked with sun-kissed blonde. She is my rock, my anchor in the storm, and I know that no matter how tough things get, she will always be by my side.

Each strike fuels my resolve as I continue to pummel the heavy bag. I know whatever awaits us in the upcoming conflict, I am ready to face it head-on. I will lead my club to victory or die trying.

Standing in the garage of the Savage Angels' clubhouse in Chicago, I can't help but feel the weight of responsibility. My brothers are gearing up for battle, and my job is to lead them through whatever hell awaits us. The intensity in the air is palpable, each man focusing solely on the task at hand.

"Hey, Dane," calls out Tank, the Chicago chapter's weapons expert, as he carefully lays out an impressive array of firepower on a long table.

"What do you think of this beauty?" He holds up a matte black AR-15, admiring it as though it is a priceless artifact.

Tank is a big bastard with arms like tree trunks and a beard that would make a Viking jealous. When it comes to guns, there isn't much he doesn't know.

"Looks damn good," I reply, my voice steady despite the knot of anxiety twisting in my gut.

I pick up the weapon and inspect it, feeling the cold metal against my skin. It is a fine piece of machinery, but I know it is not worth shit if we don't keep our heads in the game.

"Everyone, grab what you need and get ready," I bark, scanning the room as my brothers eagerly snatch up their preferred weapons.

Shotguns, pistols, knives, and even a couple of baseball bats—anything that can inflict pain and damage is fair game. We have been preparing for this showdown for weeks, and the Abruzzi family won't know what hit them. Now, it is time to show them what the Savage Angels are made of.

"Remember..." I say, catching each of their eyes in turn, "... we're a fucking family here. We watch each other's backs, and we hit them hard. Together."

"Damn right, Prez," growls Onyx. The man has a reputation that precedes him, and I would be lying if I said I didn't admire his grit. "We got your back."

"Good," I reply, a nod accompanying my words. "Now, let's get this shit done."

As the last of the weapons are secured, I can see the steely resolve etched on each of my brothers' faces. We are a formidable force with enough fire in our bellies to take on any challenge thrown our way. In this moment, I know we will prevail without a shadow of a doubt. The Savage Angels will protect their own, no matter the cost.

"Let's ride," I command, and the roar of engines fills the air as we mount our bikes.

The road ahead is uncertain, but one thing is for sure—we are ready for the fight.

CHAPTER
7

SALVATORE

"Dane!" I shout as I make my way through the garage.

He's sitting on a bike and turns, his long, dark hair tied back, a stark contrast to my slicked-back style. He's wearing jeans and a black T-shirt while I'm in a suit. We are polar opposites, and yet we are the same. Dane would do anything to protect his men and family, as would I. Being married to Emily, Dane's sister, makes him blood, but I like to think we would have become friends, even if we met as strangers.

"Sal," he grunts, acknowledging me with a nod.

"We need to talk." I glance around the room, then lower my voice. "About the situation with the Abruzzis."

"Sure," he says as he gets off the bike and leads me into an office. Shutting the door behind us, he leans against the desk and crosses his arms. "What's on your mind?"

"I want you to know I appreciate you and your men being willing to go head-to-head with the Abruzzis," I begin. "But I've been thinking... maybe there's another way."

"Another way?" Dane raises an eyebrow.

"Instead of attacking them outright, can you and the Savage Angels act as a threatening force? Intimidate them?" I ask. "I don't want you to think I'm trying to use your MC as pawns, Dane. It's just that both our families have been through enough already. We don't need more bloodshed."

Dane rubs a hand over his face. "Sal, we're all geared up and ready to roll. The men might see it as a weakness if we pull back now." He sighs and waves a hand in the air. "What did you have in mind?"

"We know, thanks to Jonas, that Don Abruzzi goes to the same restaurant once a week. It's privately owned, and years ago, the Don lent the owner money to open it. Ever since, Don Abruzzi has taken a cut. The guy has paid more than three times what he owes to the Don but has to keep paying for fear of being... taken out." I pause. "I want to keep our families and our men safe, Dane. That's all that matters."

"Go on."

"Could you and your men simply park outside the restaurant when the Don enters? A simple show of force?"

Dane pushes off the desk, his lips turning down in distaste. "We aren't puppets."

"No, you're not."

Dane is a proud man and, like me, he's worked his way up through the ranks. Our only difference is he is his men's leader, and I'm a step away from becoming the Don.

"I have the backing of the majority of the families. All I need to do is cut off the head of the snake. Don Abruzzi will not expect me to make such a bold move. Dane, my friend, my brother, I'm asking you to trust me."

He cracks his neck from side to side. "Okay."

Relief washes through me. "Thank you."

"Don't thank me yet. I've got this whole chapter ready to burn the Abruzzis to the ground. It might not be so easy to talk them down."

Before I can respond, our cell phones ring simultaneously, displaying 'Unknown' on the screens. We exchange a wary glance before answering.

"Emily?" I say, relieved to hear her voice on the other end of the line.

"Kat?" Dane's voice softens as he says his wife's name.

"I've been worried sick," Emily says, her voice filled with worry and frustration.

"I'm handling things, amare. You know I can't tell you everything," I reply, trying to keep my tone soothing but tinged with the hardness of the reality we live in.

"Dammit, Salvatore, I hate this," Emily murmurs. "I hate not knowing whether you're safe or not."

"Listen, amare, you'll be home soon," I promise, feeling the weight of her fear and concern. "Just trust me."

"Be careful," she whispers.

"Is Tony taking care of everyone?"

Emily laughs. "He says it's like herding cats, but yes, he's keeping us safe."

Her voice is the very thing I need to soothe my frayed nerves. "Is he there?"

"Yes. He said I can't talk long. In fact, he's tapping his watch. Sal, I love you. We love you. Please be careful."

Turning my back to Dane, I say, "Amare, I love you and our children more than anything. Do what Tony says."

"I will. I have to go. Be safe."

"Always," I reply, and she ends the call.

"Everything okay?" Dane asks.

"Same concerns," I admit. "But that's what we're trying to avoid, right? More danger for our families?"

"Right," he reluctantly agrees.

"How is Kat?"

Dane smiles. "Pissed at being sent away. She misses me... hell, I miss her." The smile disappears. "With Blaze and Gunner being so young, I'm missing out on all their firsts. Sending them away to protect them was the right thing to do, but fuck if I like it. This had better work, Sal," Dane warns. "Because if it doesn't, all bets are off."

"Understood," I reply. "We'll do whatever it takes to keep our families safe. You have my word."

"Good." Dane gives me a reassuring nod. "Now let's get to work."

Holding up a hand, I say, "It can't be me who kills Don Abruzzi. I want to take over his business, but according to our laws, if I kill him, I can't."

"Then who?" Dane asks.

"Lorenzo," I reply without hesitation. "He's loyal, knows how to keep his mouth shut, and he'll get the job done."

"Fine," Dane agrees. "But remember, if this goes sideways, it's on you."

"Understood," I say, extending my hand to seal our agreement.

As we shake hands, I can't help but think about the life I have chosen. The Abruzzi's are more than a crime syndicate—some of them are like family. By pursuing my current course, I hope everyone involved can see that. The Don's way of method of executing things is the old way, and we need to change for the future. I would do anything to protect those who are loyal to me, even if it means getting into bed with the devil himself.

"Let's hope this works, Sal," Dane mutters. "For all our sakes."

He opens the door and steps into the chaos of the garage. The roar of engines fills the air as his men prepare to ride out. They are ready for war, but I hope he can make them see reason.

The buzz of conversation fills Don Abruzzi's favorite restaurant as I sit at his usual table, waiting for him to arrive. My heart pounds hard, but I keep my face calm and impassive.

This is it!

The moment that will change everything.

Finally, the doors swing open, and there he is, strutting into the place like he owns it, which, in a way, he does. As soon as he steps inside, the noise dies down as if every person in the room knows what is about to happen. He scans the crowd, his eyes finally landing on me.

"Sal," he greets, his voice dripping with false

warmth as he approaches the table.

"Evening, Don Abruzzi," I reply, keeping my tone neutral.

"Do you think your friends outside scare me? Those bikers?" He chuckles.

"You underestimate them *and* me."

The Don smirks and flicks a hand in the air. "If you lay down with dogs, Sal, you'll get fleas. Or worse, put down like the mongrels they are."

He sits across from me, seemingly unfazed by the sudden silence in the restaurant. One by one, tables begin to clear out. No one speaks, but they do not need to. The message is clear. The last three tables left are occupied by the heads of the Bianchi, Santoro, and Fontana families. Each gives Don Abruzzi a two-fingered wave as they leave the restaurant, an unspoken signal to the man who has ruled them for decades.

I can see realization dawn on him, but instead of fear, he grins. "If you do this, Sal, you'll never be Don," he tells me, leaning back in his chair as if accepting his fate.

"Who said anything about *me* doing it?" I smile back, my grin deadly and cold.

In that instant, Lorenzo appears behind Don Abruzzi, swiftly wrapping a garrote around his neck. The Don's eyes widen in surprise, but there's no escaping his fate.

I watch, unflinching, as the life drains from his

face. His fingers claw at the wire, and his eyes bulge as he twists and turns, trying to escape the inevitable. Lorenzo tightens the wire, and it slices through Don Abruzzi's neck. Blood runs over the white tablecloth, turning it into a deep crimson. Lorenzo puts a knee to the Don's back, pulls harder, and with a grunt, pulls the wire all the way through to his spine. He drops the small wooden handles on the end of the wire, then spits on Don Abruzzi.

Now that it is over, I take a sip of wine, dabbing the corners of my mouth with a napkin. Standing, I pat Lorenzo on the shoulder, then make my way through the restaurant to the back door.

Night has fallen as I slide into my car. The restaurant goes up in flames, an orange glow reflecting off the windshield. I should feel relief that Don Abruzzi is dead, but all I can think about is the danger I have put my loved ones in. Some families will honor our understanding, but others won't hesitate to strike back at me or those I love.

"Fuck," I say to myself as I tightly grip the steering wheel.

The world I knew is burning before me.

There is no turning back now.

In a dimly lit room, smoke from burning cigars hangs like a thick fog. I hear the distant murmur of conversations and the clinking of whiskey glasses. Dane and I sit at a secluded table near the back, our faces partially obscured by shadows.

"Look, Dane..." my voice is low and steady. "The Abruzzis are out of the picture now, and that means there's an open seat at the table for you and your MC. But I have to warn you, the way we do things here is not the same as how it is with the Savage Angels. We have old ways, understand?"

Dane leans back in his chair, his blue eyes seemingly piercing through the haze as he considers my words. He looks like he is weighing his options, trying to figure out if this is the path he wants to take. His thoughts are hidden behind those intense eyes, but I know he will not take this choice lightly.

"Sal..." he finally speaks, his deep voice resonating throughout the room, "... I appreciate the offer, but I don't want a permanent seat at your table. My loyalty is to my MC, and that's where it's going to stay. Don't get me wrong... we'll work with you and the other families as long as my men aren't used as pawns and are paid well for their time and muscle."

I cannot help but respect the man. He knows who he is and where he stands, and there is something commendable about that. The world we live in is not black and white, and finding someone with a clear sense of identity is rare.

"Fair enough." I nod in agreement.

Deep down, I anticipated this response from him. He is a man of principle, and I respect that.

As I sip my whiskey, I cannot shake the feeling we're still walking a tightrope with danger lurking in the shadows. The Abruzzis might be gone, but there will always be someone waiting to take their place. And when that time comes, I know Dane and his MC will have my back.

"Here's to our new alliance," I say, raising my glass.

"May it never falter," Dane replies, clinking his glass against mine.

We drink together, sealing our partnership in this unpredictable world. In the back of my mind, though, I cannot help but wonder what the cost of it all will be.

Dante Fontana approaches our table. "Are you ready?"

I throw back the whiskey, stand, and straighten my white shirt.

"Let's do this."

Dante leads us into a dimly lit room, shadows dancing on the walls as whispers of smoke curl around us. I sit at the head of the table, my heart pounding in my chest. This is it, the moment I have been waiting for.

"Salvatore Agostino, do you accept the title of Don and all that comes with it?" one of the family heads asks, his voice low and steady.

"Si," I reply, feeling the weight of the responsibility settle on my shoulders.

"Then let it be known from this day forward, you are Don Salvatore Agostino." He nods, and I can feel the eyes of everyone in the room on me. Dane stands by my side, his imposing presence a reminder of the alliance we have formed.

"Congratulations, Sal," Dane says, offering a firm handshake. "I know you'll do right by your associates and ours."

"Thank you, Dane," I reply, gripping his hand tightly. It means a lot to have him here by my side, even though I know our worlds are vastly different.

As the room erupts into applause, my phone vibrates in my pocket. Pulling it out, I see Tony's name flash across the screen. My stomach clenches.

"Sorry, I need to take this." I step away from the celebration.

"Tony, what's going on?" I ask, trying to keep the anxiety from my voice.

"Sal, I can't find Kat," he pants, clearly out of breath. "I've looked everywhere, but she's just... gone."

"Shit!" I curse under my breath, panic rising in my chest. "Keep searching and call me if you find anything."

"Will do, boss," he replies before hanging up.

I stare at the phone in my hand, my mind racing with possibilities.

Dane notices my distress and approaches me with concern etched on his face. "Sal, what's wrong?" he asks, his voice tense.

"Tony just called… he can't find Kat." The words are like a punch to the gut. Dane's expression turns steely, and his eyes brim with fury.

"Let's go," he growls, already heading for the door. "We'll find her, Sal. We'll bring her home."

As we storm out of the room, leaving my crowning moment behind, I cannot help but think this is only the beginning. Our world is dangerous, and no matter how hard we try to protect our loved ones, there will always be threats lurking in the damn shadows.

CHAPTER
8

DANE

The roar of the engines vibrates through my bones as I look out the window, watching the clouds roll by like waves in the sky. The private plane is filled with Salvatore and my men, each lost in their thoughts or chatting quietly among themselves. We are flying to Hawaii, chasing leads on my wife's last-known whereabouts.

"Any news from your guys?" I ask Salvatore.

"Nothing yet," he replies, his eyes flicking back and forth between his phone's screen and the various messages coming in. "So far, no one we've talked to seems to know anything."

"Dammit," I cuss under my breath, clenching my fists in frustration.

Is Kat even still alive?

Savage Angels

Has she been taken by a rival force, or is this all some twisted ploy for power?

"We'll find her, Dane." Salvatore lays a hand on my shoulder. "I promise you. We have connections in every MC and mafia organization across the country. There's nowhere they can hide her that we won't eventually uncover."

"Let's hope you're right," I reply, my jaw tight.

We spent hours making calls, reaching out to contacts in the motorcycle club and mafia worlds. With each conversation, we employ our persuasive skills and negotiation tactics, trying to ferret out any useful information. But time and again, we come up empty.

"Hey, Prez," one of my men calls out from across the cabin, drawing my attention. "Just got word from a guy I know in the Hilo Hellions. Says they've heard whispers about someone being held at an old plantation house on the big island."

"Could be a lead, could be nothing," I say, with my heart pounding. "But we don't have any other options right now. Let's follow it up."

"I'll let the boys know we're heading to the big island," Salvatore says, already tapping out a message on his phone. "You sure you trust this guy?"

"Trust isn't the right word," I admit. "But he's never lied to me before. If he says there are whispers, then there's something going on."

As the plane continues its journey over the vast Pacific Ocean, I cannot help but feel a growing sense of unease.

What if we are too late?

What if Kat is already beyond our reach?

What if my woman is dead?

I shake off the dark thoughts and focus on what needs to be done. We have a lead, no matter how tenuous. As the president of the Savage Angels MC, I know how to navigate the treacherous waters of alliances and rivalries. And with Salvatore by my side, we will do whatever it takes to bring Kat home.

The moment we touch down on the big island, I can feel the weight of our mission pressing down on me. It is a mixture of dread and grit that settles in my gut like a shot of bad whiskey. Salvatore and I waste no time gathering our men and heading straight to the meeting location with representatives from other MCs and mafia organizations.

"Remember, these guys aren't our friends," I remind Salvatore as we walk into the warehouse.

"We're here to find Kat, not make nice."

"Understood," he replies, his eyes scanning the room for potential allies or threats.

As we enter, I notice three distinct groups gathered around makeshift tables.

The first is a group of bikers wearing cuts emblazoned with the logo of the Ares Tribe MC. Their leader, a tall, lean man with a salt-and-pepper beard, glares at us with steely gray eyes. His name is Rattlesnake, and he has a reputation for playing both sides of any deal.

The second group consists of sharply dressed men and women who stand out in stark contrast to the bikers surrounding them. They are members of the Obayashi Yakuza clan, led by a petite woman named Kiyoko. Her serene expression hides a cunning mind, one I know we need to be cautious of.

Finally, there is a group of muscular men covered in tattoos, each one bearing the mark of the Black Eclipse Syndicate. Their leader, a massive man known as Cobra, stares at us with a mix of curiosity and suspicion.

"Let's get down to business," I address the room. "We're here because somebody took my wife, Kat. We think she might be held by an individual in this room, or at least you might know where she is."

"Before we go any further..." Salvatore chimes in, "... we want to make it clear that the Savage Angels

MC and the Abruzzi Crime Family are fully prepared to show our strength and influence to protect what's ours."

"Fine words," Rattlesnake drawls skeptically. "But what do you have to offer us in return?"

"Protection," I respond, my voice as cold and hard as steel. "The Savage Angels has a lot of pull on the mainland. If you help us find Kat, we'll make sure your operations run smoothly. No turf wars, no interference."

"Same goes for the Abruzzi family," Salvatore adds. "We can provide resources, information, and muscle when needed. We're not asking you to join our fight, just help us locate my sister-in-law."

"Interesting proposition," Kiyoko says, her dark eyes appraising us carefully. "But why should we trust you? How do we know this isn't a trap or some sort of power play?"

"Because my wife's life is on the line," I growl, each word dripping with barely contained rage. "I don't give a damn about power plays. All I care about is getting her back safe and sound."

"Very well," Cobra speaks, his deep voice echoing through the warehouse. "We will consider your proposal. But know this... if we discover any deception or betrayal, there will be consequences."

"Understood," I reply, locking eyes with each leader in turn. "Now, let's work together to find Kat before it's too late."

As the negotiations continue, I cannot help but feel the ticking clock in my mind. Each moment wasted brings Kat closer to danger, closer to an unknown fate. But I cannot let that fear consume me. With Salvatore by my side and the might of the Savage Angels and Abruzzi Crime Family behind us, I know we have a fighting chance at finding her.

And I will not rest until she is back in my arms, safe and sound.

The cold metal of the gun pressed against my lower back is a constant reminder of the danger that seems to follow us like a shadow. I can feel the tension in the air, thick and heavy, as Salvatore and I face the leaders of the other MCs and mafia organizations.

"Listen ..." my voice is low and dangerous, "... we aren't here to play games or waste time. We're here because we need your help, and we're offering something in return."

"Ha!" one of them, a burly, bald man with an unkempt beard, scoffs. "And why should we trust you? How do we know this ain't just another attempt from you lot to expand your territory?"

He's one of Rattlesnake's men.

"Because it isn't about territories or power," I spit, frustration boiling within me. "It's about loyalty, and right now, my wife is in danger. And I sure as hell won't let some motherfucker lay their hands on her."

"All right, Dane," another leader, a tall woman with a snake tattoo winding around her neck, interjects skeptically. "But even if we believe you, what guarantees can you give us that working together won't turn against us eventually?"

"Listen," Salvatore chimes in, his dark eyes meeting hers. "Our families have always been about loyalty and honor. You help us find Kat, and you'll have the Savage Angels MC and Abruzzi Crime Family by your side when needed. But if we find out any of you had a hand in taking her, there will be no place for you to hide."

"Fine," Kiyoko relays. "But we still don't see how this alliance benefits us."

"Protection," I counter, my gaze unwavering. "Mutual protection. In this fucked-up world we live in, it's every man and woman for themselves. But with us, you'll have a united front. We watch each other's backs, and together, we're untouchable."

"Besides..." Salvatore adds, "... we've got resources and connections that can make all our lives easier. Weapons, information, safe havens... you name it."

"Very well," Rattlesnake finally relents, still eyeing us warily. "We'll help you find your wife, but if we even smell a hint of betrayal—"

"Then we'll deal with it accordingly," I assure him, my voice hard as steel. "But right now, let's focus on finding Kat and bringing her home."

The room is filled with nods of agreement and reluctant acceptance, but I know these small victories are enough. I need to find Kat and bring her back, no matter what it takes. And with the might of the Savage Angels MC and Abruzzi Crime Family behind me, I know I will not be fighting alone.

The room reeks of sweat, stale beer, and cigarette smoke an intoxicating mix that embodies the very essence of our underground world. I stand beside Salvatore, our backs against a graffitied wall, observing the rough crowd before us. This is the last MC we are approaching tonight, and my gut twists in anticipation.

"All right, brother..." I say under my breath, "... let's size 'em up. What do you think?"

Salvatore's eyes scan the room, analyzing each

tattooed face with expert precision. "These guys are clearly fighters and no strangers to trouble, but they're also survivors. They've got street smarts and know how to get shit done."

"Agreed." I nod, my gaze narrowing in on a scarred man with a silver nose ring. "But they lack discipline. They're reckless and impulsive. We'll need to keep a close eye on them if this alliance is going to work."

"True," Salvatore acknowledges, his tone calculating. "But if we are careful, their raw energy could be an asset. The key is to make sure they understand who's in charge."

"Damn straight." I grin, giving him a firm pat on the back. "So let's show them what the Savage Angels and Abruzzi Crime Family are all about."

As we stride across the room, the raucous laughter and chatter gradually die down, giving way to a watchful silence. Stepping into the center, I lock eyes with the scarred leader, extending my hand.

"Name's Dane Reynolds, President of the Savage Angels MC," I introduce myself, voice firm and steady. "This is Salvatore Agostino, Don of the Abruzzi Crime Family."

"Jax," the leader grunts, shaking my hand with a crushing grip. "So, what brings the infamous Dane Reynolds and Salvatore Agostino to our humble abode?"

Savage Angels

"An alliance," Salvatore replies, never one to mince words. "One that benefits us all."

Jax eyes us warily, clearly weighing his options. "And how do you plan on making that happen?"

"Simple," I say, leaning in close. "We combine our strengths, your ferociousness and street smarts with our discipline and connections. Together, we'll be a force to be reckoned with."

"Besides..." Salvatore interjects, "... we've got each other's backs. In this fucked-up world, loyalty is everything."

A slow smile spreads across Jax's scarred face, and he gives me a firm handshake, his grip like iron. "You've got yourself a deal, Reynolds. Welcome to the family."

As the room erupts into cheers and clinking beer bottles, I allow myself a moment of satisfaction, knowing we have taken another step toward finding Kat and bringing her home. United, there is no enemy we cannot face and no challenge we will not overcome. And with my brothers by my side, I feel invincible.

"Here's to new alliances," I shout over the noise, raising my bottle high. "To loyalty, strength, and new friends!"

"Brotherhood!" the room roars back, our voices joined together in defiance and camaraderie.

For tonight, at least, we are one, and nothing will tear us apart.

Pulling up in front of the safe house, I glance at Sal, but his eyes are glued to the front door. It opens, and Tony is the first person out, followed by Emily and Sal's children. I open the car door as Jesse and Kristen emerge.

"Dad!" Jesse yells as he runs toward me and wraps himself around my leg. My hand goes to the top of his head, and I ruffle his hair. Kristen holds back, her eyes scanning the interior of the car.

"Is Mom with you?"

Looking at Tony, I shake my head. "No, princess. We're still looking for her." Tony hangs his head and walks back inside the house.

Emily hugs me. "Tony has been beating himself up ever since Kat went missing. It's not his fault, Dane."

I glance at Sal and nod once. Rehashing what should and should not have happened won't bring my wife back. Bending, I pick up Kristen and put Jesse's hand in mine. "Come on, you two, I'm starving, and I want to know what you've been doing here in paradise."

"Uncle Truth says you're going to get Mommy back. You will, won't you, Dad?" asks Kristen.

I walk them inside the house. "Where is your room?"

Jesse tugs on my hand. "Up the stairs." He runs ahead, and I follow him.

The house is a blend of sleek lines and Hawaiian architecture. Massive windows showcase the Pacific Ocean. Jesse opens a door, runs, and sits on a bed. Still with Kristen in my arms, I sit next to him and position her on my lap as I drape an arm around him.

"We will find your mom, I promise. But until we do, I need you to be strong for me."

Jesse tilts his little head to the side. "For you, Dad?" he asks.

"Yeah. Sometimes daddies need help too."

Kristen puts her arms around my neck and squeezes.

"Do you like our room, Dad?" asks Jesse.

The room has two single beds separated by a bedside table. On it is a book with a bookmark sticking out of it.

"Yeah, bud. What are you reading?"

"Mom was reading us *Charlotte's Web*."

My heart skips a beat. Kat loves reading to the kids. "How about tonight I pick up where she left off?"

Kristen shakes her head. "You don't do the voices."

"Yeah, Dad, Mom does the voices," Jesse says.

"How about I try to do the voices?"

Kristen leans back to look in my face. "Promise?"

"Promise."

Jesse asks, "Mom won't mind, will she?"

Hugging my children tight, I say, "No, bud, she won't mind at all."

The sun dips below the horizon, painting the sky with hues of red and orange as I stand on the edge of a rocky cliff overlooking the ocean. The wind whips through my hair, carrying with it the salty scent of the sea. It is a beautiful sight but one that brings me no comfort. Despite our efforts, Kat remains lost to us. The gnawing worry in the pit of my stomach grows more insistent with each passing day.

"Any news?" I ask Salvatore, who has been on his cell phone for the past hour, making calls to every contact he can think of.

"Nothing yet," he replies, frustration evident in his voice. "But we're not giving up, Dane. We'll find her."

I clench my fists at my side, feeling helpless for the first time in my life. "She's out there somewhere, Sal. And I won't rest until I bring her home."

"Come, my friend. Blaze and Gunner are awake. It will do you good to spend time with your children."

Turning, we walk back inside the house. Sitting at the dining table is Dave, Kat's manager, and his partner, Luther. They each have one of my children in their arms. Dave is cooing at Blaze and stops when he sees me.

"Hello, Dane. Do you want to hold your son?" asks Dave.

"Yes."

He stands and passes Blaze to me, and I sit beside Luther so I might stare at both my sons.

Jesse comes in and sits opposite me, grinning at his brothers. "Truth says they look like Mom."

"They do."

"Do I?"

"You and your sister are a mix of us both. You have my eyes and your mom's mouth."

"Which means I do too," says Kristen as she climbs onto the chair beside her brother.

"Yep." I smile at her.

"I miss Mom." Kristen's mouth quivers, and my heart breaks for her.

"I swear on my life, we will bring your mom home. We're a family, and nothing can tear us apart."

"Family," Jesse echoes, his voice strong despite the tears that threatened to spill.

"Family," Kristen agrees as she walks around the table and holds me close.

"Family," Salvatore affirms, placing a hand on my shoulder.

"Family," I whisper, gazing at my children with renewed resolve.

With every beat of my heart, I vow to find Kat and reunite our loved ones, no matter what it takes.

CHAPTER
9

KATARINA SAUNDERS
Lead Guitarist in The Grinders
and Dane Reynold's Wife
Past Event

My toes sink in the warm sand while the sun kisses my skin. It is a perfect day in Hawaii, surrounded by my children and the other members of The Grinders. Laughter fills the air as we splash around in the turquoise water, the salt spray cooling our faces. Tony is annoyed at us for leaving the safe house, but we need a break. The beach is filled with tourists, and no one pays as much attention. The only one of us who doesn't blend in is Tony because he's constantly scanning the people around us and looking for possible threats.

"Hey, Mom!" my son, Jesse, calls out, tossing a

beach ball my way. I catch it effortlessly, grinning at him before sending it back with a gentle push.

"Nice catch, Kat!" Jamie, our drummer, shouts.

We are a family bonded by our love for music and each other.

But even though we need this time to relax, I cannot shake the feeling that danger is lurking just beneath the surface. Our fame has brought us incredible opportunities, but it has also attracted dark forces that threaten to tear it all away. Every stranger could be an enemy, every passerby a potential threat. I know I have to stay vigilant, not just for me but for my bandmates.

"Hey, babe." Jasmin flops down beside me. "You seem a little tense. Everything okay?"

Forcing a smile, I try to keep my fears hidden. "Just soaking it all in, you know? We've worked so hard to get here, and I don't want to take it for granted."

"Never," she replies. "We'll keep this dream alive together."

As we watch our children play in the surf, I cannot help but feel uneasy. Without Dane, I don't feel safe.

"Hey, Kat, you wanna grab some lunch?" Jamie asks, gesturing toward a nearby food truck. "I'm starving."

"Sure," I reply, my gaze scanning the crowd for any signs of danger. "Let's just keep an eye on the kids, okay?"

"Of course," he replies, understanding the underlying message in my words.

Tony nods at me and stays with the children, his gaze fixed on them as Jamie and I walk to the food truck. I cannot shake the nagging feeling that someone is watching us. The eyes of potential predators seem to lurk behind every pair of sunglasses, and every smile holds sinister intentions. With each step, I know the battle to protect my everyone I love has only just begun. Both of us are wearing hats and sunglasses to protect our identity, but if someone should recognize us, our anonymity will be blown.

"Cool, they've got tacos. How many do you think Blair will eat?"

Blair is our saxophonist. He is six foot four and built like a linebacker.

"The whole truck."

Jamie chuckles. "I'm thinking three for each of the guys, two for the girls, and one each for the kids."

"I'd go four for the guys, three for the girls, and one each for the kids."

Jamie laughs louder. "You're going to bankrupt me."

"Didn't realize it was your treat. Don't forget drinks for everyone."

He shakes his head at me and places the order

with the food truck. The person taking the order looks shocked. While we wait for our food and drinks, I look around at the people near me. The feeling that someone is watching me sends a chill down my spine, but no one is paying us any special attention.

It takes the cook about half an hour to do our order. Blair wanders over just as they are putting our tacos into bags.

"Of course, you arrive after the food has been paid for, and all we need to do is carry it back," chides Jamie.

Blair feigns innocence, picks up a bag, and carries it back to the beach.

"I swear, he has the first dollar we ever made." Jamie shakes his head.

"Probably. Remember, Blair came from nothing."

Jamie laughs. "Didn't we all?"

Linking my arm through his, I say, "Yes. And look at us now. Hiding out in one of the most beautiful places on the planet with a cranky Italian who wants to keep us cooped up in a mansion twenty-four-seven."

The smile falls off Jamie's face. "We were having so much fun, I'd forgotten. Come on, safety in numbers."

Jamie walks me back to my friends. Dave and Luther are under an umbrella, each with a baby in their arms. Dane and Salvatore are the only ones missing from what would be a great family vacation.

Gulping down the last bite of my fish taco, I cannot shake the feeling someone is still watching me. My eyes dart around, trying to find the source of my unease. A chill runs down my spine despite the warm Hawaiian sun.

A woman is standing not too far from us, and although she doesn't look familiar, she appears to be watching us closely.

"Kat?" Truth questions, following my gaze.

"I think we are busted."

"Yeah, she's watching us like a hawk. Time to go."

The woman's face twists into a scowl.

Truth holds out a hand and tugs me to my feet.

"Jesse, Kristen, time to go."

"About time," scolds Tony, the only person on the beach wearing long pants and a jacket. He's carrying a gun, but he doesn't even try to blend in.

"Everyone, pack up," Tony orders the rest of the group. "We're leaving."

The woman walks toward me. "Kat," she calls out, stopping us in our tracks.

"Stay away from me and mine," I say, trying to keep my voice steady. "We're on holiday and don't need the press. I'm sorry, but this isn't a good time for a fan."

"Kat, please," she continues, stepping toward us. "I just want to talk."

Shaking my head, I pick up our towels and move away from her.

"Please, hear me out," she insists, her gaze unwavering.

The closer she comes, the more I realize how truly dangerous this situation is, and I do not want her any closer to my family.

"Tony, get everyone out of here. I'll talk to her... you get them to the cars."

"I don't like this," he warns.

"You can see me. I'll be fine. We're in public, after all."

Tony takes a deep breath, nods once, and herds everyone toward the cars. They move around a parked van and disappear from my sight.

"Kat," she whispers again, but her voice has changed—it is cold, determined.

Now she's within a couple of feet of me, and there's something about her, something familiar.

"Do I know you?"

The woman nods and tilts her head to the side. "I killed Gareth for you."

"Stella?"

She nods, but this woman looks nothing like the person I knew. Hell, she's had so much plastic surgery her mother wouldn't know her.

Stella reaches me, grabs my arm, and twists it behind my back, forcing me to my knees. The pain is intense.

"What the fuck do you want from me?"

"Quiet," Stella hisses, her grip tightening on my wrist. "I'm doing this for your own good, Kat. You need me."

"Need you?" I spit out, struggling against her iron grip. "You're fucking insane!"

Stella's other hand shoots out, gripping my hair and yanking my head back, forcing me to look into her dark, unyielding eyes. "You have no idea what I've done for you. What I've sacrificed…"

"Let me go, you crazy bitch!" I snarl, attempting to kick her, but she easily dodges the attack, keeping me pinned to the ground.

"Shut up and listen!" Stella demands, her voice shaking with barely contained fury. "Everything I've done is to protect you, Kat. You're in danger, and you don't even realize it!"

"Protect me?" I scoff, the absurdity of her claim fueling my anger. "By kidnapping me and terrorizing my family?"

"Your so-called 'family' is the reason you're in danger," Stella growls, dragging me to my feet by my hair. "You need to see things clearly, and I'm going to make sure that happens."

She presses a gun into my spine, and as she drags me away. All I can think about is how desperately I need to protect those I love, but for now, I am trapped at the mercy of a madwoman who claims to be my savior.

"Please," I whisper, my voice cracking with fear and desperation. "Just let me go…"

"Never," Stella replies, her grip on me unrelenting as we disappear into the crowd of people near where we were spending the day.

Thoughts of escape run through my mind, but with Stella having a gun, I won't put anyone in danger.

CHAPTER 10

KAT
Present

The stench of rotting garbage and stale cigarette smoke assaults my nostrils as I blink my eyes open, trying to adjust to the dim light. The room is filthy, a dingy hole that barely resembles a habitable space. The walls are stained with grime and peeling paint, and the only furniture is a single rickety wooden chair with Stella sitting on it, watching me.

"Awake now, princess?" Stella asks, her cold eyes locked onto mine. "About time you faced reality."

"Reality?" I spit, my heart thudding in my chest. "You're fucking delusional, Stella."

"Me? Delusional?" She laughs, a bitter sound that sends chills down my spine. "I'm the one trying to save your sorry ass."

"Save me?" I hiss, desperately scanning the room for anything I can use to escape. A broken windowpane catches my attention but is too small to squeeze through. "From what, exactly?"

"From them," Stella replies cryptically, her gaze unwavering. "Your precious Grinders ain't what they seem, Kat."

"Shut up," I snarl, refusing to let her words get under my skin. "You don't know anything about them."

"Wrong." Stella leans in closer, her eyes daring me to challenge her. "I've been watchin' you all for years, sweetheart. I know more than you think."

"Stalking people doesn't make you an expert, Stella," I retort, my pulse racing as I try to figure out a way to break free from my restraints. My wrists are bound tightly behind my back with a coarse rope that digs into my skin, and my head throbs from being pistol-whipped into unconsciousness. I need to get away from this lunatic before she does something even more drastic.

"Call it what you want." Stella shrugs, her expression chillingly calm. "But I've seen the danger you're in, and I won't let anything happen to you."

"Your fucked-up obsession doesn't give you the right to kidnap me," I spit out, struggling against the ropes as quietly as possible.

"Sometimes people need to be saved from

themselves," she replies smugly, leaning back in her chair and watching me with predatory eyes. "It's my job to open your eyes, Kat. Whether you like it or not."

"Go to hell," I mutter, my heart pounding as I feel the rope around my wrists loosen ever so slightly.

"Been there, done that," Stella quips, a twisted grin spreading across her face. "Now, let's see if we can make you see the light."

As she stands, I brace myself for whatever twisted lesson she has planned. But one thing is certain—I am not going down without a fight.

Stella's eyes flicker with a volatile mix of emotions, her gaze boring into me like a drill. I have never felt so vulnerable, but I cannot afford to show fear. I have to keep my wits about me if I am going to escape.

"Y'know, Kat," she says casually, the sudden calm in her voice more unsettling than her previous outbursts. "I did you a favor once. Killed that bastard, Gareth Goodman, for you and Will Van Ryken. Gave him a drug overdose in the hospital. Made it look like suicide."

My stomach churns at her words, bile rising in my throat. "You sick fuck," I say, unable to contain my disgust.

I need to stay focused on finding a way out of this hellhole, but the thought of Stella murdering someone in cold blood fills me with rage.

"Aw, don't be like that," Stella coos mockingly. "You should be grateful. He was a threat to you, after all." Her voice is as smooth as silk, trying to lull me into a false sense of security, but her expression darkens. "And now I'm the only one who can protect you."

"Protect me?" I snort, adrenaline coursing through my veins. "From what? My shadow?"

"From people who want to hurt you, sweetheart. People like Gareth, who would've been all too happy to see you suffer." There is a twisted sincerity in her words, sending shivers down my spine.

As she speaks, I catalog every item in the filthy room, searching for anything that might help me break free. My attention settles on a rusty pipe in the corner, just within reach of my bound feet. If I could somehow maneuver it toward me, maybe I could use it to cut through the ropes.

"Nice try, sweetheart," Stella sneers, clearly noticing my gaze. "But you're not getting out of here that easily."

"Fuck you." My heart pounds as I try to come up with another plan.

"Feisty. I like it," she says, a sinister grin spreading across her face. "But it won't do you any good."

"Listen, Stella," I begin, trying to appeal to any shred of humanity left in her. "I don't know what twisted shit is going on in your head, but this isn't the way to help me. Let me go, and we can figure this out together."

"Nice try, Kat." She smirks, her eyes narrowing. "But I'm not falling for your tricks. You're staying right here until *you* see the truth."

"Truth? What truth?" I demand, desperation creeping into my voice. "All I see is a crazy bitch who's lost her fucking mind! Whatever delusions you have about protecting me, they're not doing anyone any good." I try to keep my voice steady despite the fear coursing through me. "You've killed two men already. How many more lives do you want on your conscience?"

"Conscience?" Stella chuckles darkly. "You think I feel guilty for ridding the world of filth like Gareth? He was a parasite, and so was Ryken. They were holding you back, Kat."

"Dammit, Stella! You don't get to decide that!" I shout, anger momentarily overpowering my fear.

"Watch me," she replies coldly, her gaze unwavering.

I know I need to act fast before Stella's next outburst, or worse, she decides to make good on her threats. My eyes dart around the room again, frantically searching for something, anything that could help me escape.

"You know, Stella..." I begin, hoping to stall her while I formulate a plan. "Maybe we could work together. If you're so intent on keeping me safe, there has to be a way that doesn't involve kidnapping and murder."

"Ha!" Stella barks, her laughter tinged with bitterness. "I didn't expect you to understand, but I hoped you might try. Besides, I haven't killed anyone this time. Although that older man who's been looking after you, he's a problem. Do you know he works for Salvatore Agostino? Word on the street is he's the new head of the Abruzzi Crime Family." She laughs and shakes her head. "Guess it's called the Agostino Crime Family now."

Not having a clue what she is talking about, I say nothing as she does a weird little dance and talks to herself as she twirls around the room.

At that moment, I see my chance. As Stella's focus wavers, I catch sight of a shard of glass from a broken bottle mixed in with the rubbish on the floor. With all the strength I can muster, I swing my legs forward, hoping to crawl across the floor and somehow get to the piece of broken glass.

"Nice try, Kat," Stella snarls, lunging toward me.

Yet, speed is on my side. Clutching the shard tightly, I carve through the ropes binding my wrists. The moment they loosen, I scramble to my feet and lunge at Stella, catching her off guard.

"Get off me, you bitch!" she screams, but I do not relent. We struggle, our bodies colliding with the grime-covered walls as we fight for control. Pain surges through me as Stella's nails dig into my flesh, but sheer adrenaline fuels my resolve to overpower her.

Finally, I manage to pin Stella's arms beneath her, using my knee to keep her down. Her eyes burn with rage, her breath coming in ragged gasps.

"Give it up, Stella." I pant, my breath heavy. "I won't let you hurt anyone else."

"Bold words from someone who's still very much in danger," she taunts, a wicked grin twisting her lips.

Before I can react, Stella bucks her hips violently, throwing me off balance. I tumble to the floor, losing my grip on her. My heart races as I try to scramble back to my feet, knowing every second counts if I am to make my escape.

But as I reach for the door handle, I hesitate, my mind plagued by a nagging question. Would Stella regain control and continue her twisted mission of protection? Or will I find a way to put an end to her reign of terror once and for all?

The answer hangs heavy in the air as the door creaks open, revealing the uncertain darkness beyond.

CHAPTER
11

EMILY

The warm night air wafts over my skin as I stand on the porch, looking out into the darkness. The wind whispers through the trees, a haunting lullaby only matched by the unease in my gut. My thoughts race with memories of days gone by, sacrifices made, and the dangerous world in which we are now firmly entrenched.

"Amare," Salvatore's voice breaks through the silence like shattering glass, pulling me back to the present. He wraps his arms around me from behind, his warmth driving away the chill that has crept up my spine. "I have something for you."

He hands me a small box. Its matte-black surface reflects the pale moonlight as I turn it over in my hands. I can feel the weight of his gaze on me, anticipation mingling with the faintest hint of vulnerability.

"Open it," he urges softly, his breath warm against my ear.

My fingers fumble with the lid, curiosity overwhelming the cold dread that has settled in my chest. As I lift the top, I find a delicate gold chain nestled within the folds of midnight velvet. A small key dangles from the chain, its intricate design shimmering in the moonlight.

"Sal..." I breathe out, tears prickling at the corners of my eyes. "It's beautiful."

"It's a symbol, amare," he explains, his voice thick with emotion. "A reminder that you hold the key to this family and our future. No matter what happens, no matter how deep we're in, you and the children keep me going. You're my rock, amare."

Tears stream down my cheeks, their trails burning hot against my skin. I turn to face him, our gazes locked in a moment of raw, unspoken understanding.

"Sal, I've been thinking about all the things we've given up for each other," I whisper, my voice cracking under the weight of the words. "The life I left behind when I married you, the risks you take every day to protect us... it isn't easy, but I wouldn't trade it for anything."

"Neither would I, amare," he murmurs, pressing a tender kiss against my forehead. "We have each other's backs, no matter what. That's what love is, right?"

I nod, my heart swelling with gratitude and sorrow as I look into his eyes, dark pools that mirror the storm brewing within me. We are in this together, bound by love and loyalty, even as the world threatens to tear us apart.

"Sal..." I hesitate, unsure whether to voice the fears that haunt me. "Are we ever going to be free from all this? Can our kids have a future outside of the Abruzzi Crime Family?"

"Emily, we'll find a way," he promises, his hand tightening around mine as if to seal the vow. "No matter what it takes, I'll make sure our children can choose their own path in life. They won't be forced into this darkness."

His words wrap around me like a shield, offering some measure of comfort amidst the chaos surrounding us. As we cling to each other on the windswept porch, I pray to whatever gods might be listening that Salvatore's promise can stand against the maelstrom waiting just beyond the horizon.

The night is tense as I watch Dane pace back and

forth in the dimly lit living room. His eyes are glued to his phone, waiting for any word about Kat's whereabouts. He looks like a caged tiger, restless and ready to pounce at the first sign of danger.

"Sal," I whisper, turning to my husband standing by my side, his face a mask of concern. "I can't take this anymore. We need a break, just for a moment."

"All right, amare. Let's go upstairs," Salvatore's voice is low and steady, like a lifeline amidst the storm.

As we reach the top of the stairs, he pulls me into him, his lips crashing down onto mine with a passion that takes my breath away. Our tongues dance together, reigniting the spark we have always had, even in these dark times. I feel his strong arms wrap around me, and it is like coming home.

"Salvatore," I gasp as he carries me to our bedroom, his hard body pressed against mine, promising a sweet release from the unbearable tension.

He throws me onto the bed, and I wriggle out of my clothes as he strips off his own. The sight of his chiseled muscles, glistening with perspiration, sends a shiver of desire through me.

"Emily," he growls, his voice deep and primal as he climbs onto the bed, positioning himself between my legs. "You're all I need... you and our children."

His words are like a spark igniting a fire within me that burns with an intensity surpassing even the brightest sun. Sal trails kisses from my mouth down my body to my inner thigh. I moan in frustration as I try to guide him between my legs.

"So greedy." Sal chuckles.

"I've missed you," I purr.

His mouth closes over my clit, and he sucks. My body arches, and a long, loud moan escapes me.

"More," I plead.

As a lover, Sal never disappoints. He's never once left me wanting. But this is the longest we have ever been apart, so I know he must want to be inside me to reach his own bliss.

Sal inserts a finger and then another as his tongue laps at me. I'm concentrating, searching for the thread of desire that will push me over the edge when Sal removes his fingers, only to slowly work his whole hand back inside me. With his tongue applying pressure to my clit, he moves his fist slowly, and I feel my thighs begin to burn.

So damn good.

Spreading my legs wider, I move my hips to increase the pressure. My hands grip his head to hold him in place as I ride his face.

The orgasm hits me hard.

I arch off the bed and moan out his name over and over as wave after wave of pleasure courses through me. Sal doesn't stop until every last quiver is wrung from my body. He removes his hand, and I gasp at the sudden loss of fullness. Sal's mouth closes over my nipple as he thrusts into me. I feel every inch of his hard, muscled body pressing against mine, filling me up again, hitting just right and driving me wild with pleasure. Our bodies move in perfect harmony, our passion building with each beat of our hearts.

"Sal!" My voice echoes through the room as my body reaches its peak a second time.

I'm in pure ecstasy. This man knows exactly how to draw out the electrifying sensations which dance across my skin and pussy. The world around us fades away, leaving only the two of us entwined in a frenzy of desire and need.

"Emily," he whispers breathlessly into my ear as he grunts loudly, embedding himself within me. "Mine," Sal growls out as he spills his seed inside me. We collapse onto the bed, our bodies entwined and slick with sweat. "I will always love you."

And at this moment, I know it is true. His love for me is what keeps me going through these dark times, and in his arms, I find solace and comfort unlike anything else in this world.

The following evening, I walk into our bedroom to find a sumptuous feast laid out on the bed. Candles flicker in the dim room, casting shadows that dance along the walls, creating an intimate haven just for the two of us.

"Salvatore... you did this?" I ask, tears filling my eyes at the unexpected gesture.

"Of course, amare," he says with a grin, pulling me close. "We need moments like this to remember what we're fighting for."

As we sit to eat, the outside world fades away, replaced by the comforting presence of my husband and his love for me—a beacon of light amidst the chaos.

"Sal," I whisper between bites of pasta, his hand caressing mine tenderly. "Thank you for this. It means everything to me."

"Anything for you, Emily," he replies. His eyes fill with warmth and devotion. And for once, I allow myself to believe we can weather any storm so long as we have each other.

The flickering candlelight casts a warm glow over the room, making it feel like we are the only two people left in this godforsaken world. I lean back against Salvatore's chest, his arms wrap protectively around me, and I let out a shaky breath.

"Sal... I'm scared," I admit, my voice barely a whisper as I stare into the dancing flames. "This life... it's taken so much from us already. What if it takes even more?"

"Amare, I know. I'm scared too," he confesses, his voice rough with emotion. He presses a tender kiss on the top of my head. "I never wanted to bring any of this shit down on you or our kids."

His words hang heavily between us, and for a moment, we sit in silence, the air thick with unspoken fears and regrets.

"Things have changed, Emily," he continues, his grip on me tightening ever so slightly. "I'm now the head of the Abruzzi Crime Family. I know I promised you I'd try to get us out, but now... we're in deeper than ever."

My stomach twists painfully at his words, the future suddenly looking darker than it had a moment ago. My heart races as I think of Vincent, our oldest, and the path that awaits him.

"Sal... what does this mean for us... our family?" I ask, my voice trembling. "Vincent... do you expect him to follow in your footsteps?"

Salvatore's body stiffens behind me, and he lets out a ragged sigh before suddenly pulling away. He drops to his knees in front of me, his eyes begging for understanding.

"Emily, listen to me," he pleads, his hands gripping mine tightly. "I swear to you, none of our children will ever be part of this life. They'll make their own way in the world, free from this darkness.

I promise I'll protect all of you at any cost."

His sincerity shines in his eyes, and I want so desperately to believe him. I manage to smile and nod, even though my heart still aches with worry.

"Thank you, Sal," I whisper, my tears threatening to spill over.

But as he holds me close once more, I can't shake the sense that something has fundamentally shifted between us. The man I'd fallen in love with, the rebellious, passionate soul who won my heart, is now the Don of one of the most powerful crime families in the world.

And no matter how much we love each other, I fear the path we are on will only lead us further into the darkness.

CHAPTER 12

KAT

Outside this filthy room, I look left, then right, when Stella lunges at me. Her hand clamps over my mouth with a rag. A sickly sweet scent fills my nostrils, and I struggle to break free, but she is too strong. My lungs grow heavy, and darkness swallows me whole.

"St... Stella," I manage before everything goes black.

My head throbs and I feel disoriented as I open my eyes. The air tastes salty, and I hear waves crashing in the distance. I try to sit up and discover one of my wrists is handcuffed to a rusty pipe. Shuffling around on the mattress on the floor, I awkwardly make it into a sitting position.

"Fuck," I say to myself, tugging at the cuffs. Pain

shoots up my arm, but they don't budge.

"Stella!" I yell, my voice echoing through the room. "Where the hell am I?"

There is no answer, only the relentless sound of the ocean and the faint cry of gulls outside. The place is cleaner than where she'd kept me before, almost sterile. But there is no sign of Stella.

"Stella!" I scream again. "Let me go, you crazy bitch!"

My heart pounds in my chest, and I can feel panic rising like bile in my throat.

What has she done to me?

What does she want?

"Please..." I whisper, tears streaming down my face. "My children need me."

But the room remains silent, save for the distant call of the ocean, and I know no one is coming to rescue me.

Gritting my teeth, I yank hard on the handcuffs, trying to free myself from their steel grip. My wrist screams in pain as the metal digs into my skin, drawing blood. With every futile attempt, I can feel my hope slipping away like sand through my fingers.

"Fuck!" I yell, the sound bouncing off the walls mocking me. A feeling of utter hopelessness settles over me. I am trapped.

The door creaks open, revealing Stella—her silhouette is framed by the dim light seeping in from the hallway. She steps inside, carrying a tray with food and a bottle of water. Her expression is calm, almost serene, a stark contrast to the chaos that rages within me.

"Thought you might be hungry," she says casually, setting the tray on a nearby table. "You're going to need your strength."

"Go to hell!" I hiss. "Let me go, Stella. This *isn't* you."

"Isn't it?" she asks, arching an eyebrow as she sits across from me. Gone are the wild eyes and manic energy I'd seen before. She seems more relaxed now, more in control of herself. It is unnerving as hell.

"Please," I whisper, my voice cracking. "My family needs me. Don't do this."

She studies me for a moment, those eyes piercing through me like ice. Then she sighs and takes a sip of water.

"We'll see," she says, her voice devoid of emotion. "For now, eat something. You look like shit."

As much as I hate to admit it, I am starving. But there is no way in hell I am giving her the satisfaction of seeing me break. So I just glare, defiance burning in my chest like a fire that refuses to be extinguished.

"Suit yourself," Stella says with a shrug, standing up and heading for the door. "But it's only going to get harder from here."

With those chilling words, she leaves me alone once more. Clenching my jaw, the cold metal of the handcuffs bite into my wrist as I tug at them uselessly. My heart pounds relentlessly, my only thought is to escape and get back to those I love.

"Stella, listen to me," I say loudly, trying to keep my voice steady despite the fear constricting my throat. "You don't understand what you're doing here. Dane, my husband... he's not going to stop until he finds me. And our kids... they need their mother. You remember Jesse and Kristen, right? You know how much they mean to me."

The door opens a crack, then fully opens. Stella leans against the door frame, and I search her face for any sign of humanity, any glimmer of the person she used to be. But her eyes are cold and distant, as if a part of her has been lost somewhere along the way.

"Then there are Blaze and Gunner," I continue, desperation creeping into my voice. "Did you know I had twin boys? They're only babies, Stella, and they won't understand where their mother is. They'll think I've abandoned them."

Stella seems to waver for a moment, her icy gaze flickering with something that almost resembles compassion. But just as quickly, it disappears as her lips turn down, and she shrugs.

"Kat..." Stella whispers, her voice barely audible.

"I know you care about them. I know you love your family with all your heart. But sometimes... sometimes we have to make sacrifices."

"Is that what this is?" I ask as my anger flares within me. "Some twisted sacrifice? You're tearing my life apart, Stella! Don't you see?"

"Maybe one day you'll understand," she murmurs, her eyes locked onto mine with an intensity I can't quite decipher. "Until then, just know I'm doing what I have to do."

"Please," I beg, my vision blurring with unshed tears. "Let me go. Let me get back to my children."

Stella hesitates for a heartbeat, and, in this moment, I dare to hope that maybe, just maybe, she will let me go. But the fleeting flicker of compassion vanishes once more, leaving only the cold, hard resolve of a woman who has been pushed too far.

"Sorry, Kat," she whispers, turning away from me. "I can't do that."

"Think about my kids, Stella," I choke out. "They're going to be so scared without me. You wouldn't want them to worry, would you?"

Her eyes flicker with uncertainty, but she doesn't respond right away. My heart hammers in my chest as I watch her wrestle with her conscience, desperately hoping she'd find it within herself to let me go.

"Kat..." Stella finally says. "I know... I know how much your kids mean to you. And I don't want them to suffer. But…" She hesitates, then sighs heavily. "I can't risk going to jail, Kat. You know too much. You know about Will Van Ryken and everything else."

"Stella, please…" I plead, straining against the handcuffs that bind me to the cold, unforgiving pipe. "I won't say anything. I swear. Just let me go."

Stella shakes her head, the gesture filling me with dread. "I'm sorry, Kat. I just can't take that chance." Her voice is thick with regret, but her resolve remains unshaken.

"Dammit, Stella!" I shout, frustration and desperation boiling over. "You used to be one of us. You lived at the Savage Angels clubhouse, you sat at our table! How could you do this to me? To all of us?"

"Things change, Kat." She turns away from me. "Sometimes we have no choice but to do what's necessary."

"Even if it destroys everything? Even if it hurts the people we care about?" Tears burn the corners of my eyes.

"Especially then," she whispers.

"Listen, Stella, I promise you, I won't say a word about any of this. Hell, I'll even go with you to the police station and tell them it was all just a big misunderstanding."

She eyes me warily, and it's then I notice she has a rag in her hand and is playing with the edges of it. *Is it the same one she used to knock me out?*

"You'd really do that?" she asks, a hint of skepticism creeping into her tone.

"Of course," I reply, trying to inject as much sincerity as I can muster. "I only want to go home, Stella. And I don't want you to throw your life away, either. Let's put an end to all this madness, yeah?"

Stella hesitates, her face a whirlwind of emotions—doubt, fear, hope. Finally, she nods, but something is lurking behind her eyes that sets off alarm bells in my head.

"All right, Kat," she agrees, her voice barely above a whisper. "I'll let you go. But remember, if you break your promise, there will be consequences."

"Deal!" I swallow hard against the unease snaking up my spine.

As Stella moves closer to unlock the handcuffs, I cannot help but wonder what lies hidden beneath the surface of her calm demeanor. My instincts scream at me to be cautious, but with no other options available, I have no choice but to trust in the fragile truce we have established.

"Thanks, Stella," I say as the cold metal finally falls away from my wrist, leaving an angry red mark behind. "I won't forget what you've done for me today."

"Let's just hope you keep your end of the bargain," she replies, her eyes never leaving mine as she steps back, the distance between us feeling far more significant than mere inches.

"Let's go." I force a shaky smile onto my face. "The sooner we clear this up, the better."

Together, we walk out of this dismal room, and as we step into the harsh light of day, I fight the urge to run. Stella has overpowered me twice, and I have no desire to be taken prisoner by her a third time. Her eyes rarely leave me, and when we climb into the car, I sigh in relief.

Hopefully, she will drive me somewhere where people are milling about, and I can signal someone for help.

The car hums beneath us as Stella navigates the busy streets, her eyes flicking between the rearview mirror and the road ahead. My heart pounds in my chest with every bump we hit.

"Almost there," Stella mutters under her breath, her knuckles white on the steering wheel.

I squint against the harsh sunlight filtering through the windshield, catching a glimpse of a man on a motorcycle across the street. He seems to be watching us, and I can't help but notice the ink-black tattoos snaking up his arms.

Stella glances at the biker for a moment before her face hardens, her grip on the steering wheel tightening even further. "Shit. Obayashi Yakuza. We need to move."

Stella guns the engine, weaving through traffic with a newfound urgency.

My stomach churns with each swerve and brake, my mind racing as I try to make sense of how I ended up in this mess and how I am going to get out of it.

"Here," Stella says suddenly, then slams on the brakes and pulls over to the side of the road. "Police station's just around the corner. You should go."

"Wait, what?" Panic surges through me. "What are you going to do?"

"I'll be fine," she replies, her voice steady. "I've got some things to take care of."

"Stella..." I swallow hard. "He could be anyone. Come with me to the police station."

"Kat, I..." She pauses, her gaze locked with mine for a heartbeat before she reaches over and pushes open the passenger door. "I'll always be watching. I will do everything I can to protect you... always."

Not wanting her to change her mind, I quickly get out of the car. Whatever crazy thoughts she has running through her head, Stella thinks the guy on the bike is a threat. I glance at him, but he is sitting in traffic, not paying Stella or me much attention.

"Go on. And remember... this was all just a

misunderstanding," Stella urges.

My heart pounds in my chest as Stella gets out of the car, her gun hanging from her hand. I immediately begin to walk backward away from her, scared she's going to kill me. Instead, she approaches the man on the motorcycle, gun raised.

"Stella, no!" I scream.

The man is too quick, pulling out his weapon and firing before Stella pulls the trigger. The shot rings out like a thunderclap, echoing through the street. Time seems to slow, and I watch in horror as the bullet tears through Stella's head, blood and gore erupting like a grotesque fountain.

People on the street scatter like frightened birds, and screams fill the air as they run for cover. My scream feels lodged in my throat, a strangled sob of disbelief and pain.

I turn to run, desperate to get away from the nightmare that has unfolded before me, but before I can take more than a few steps, a strong arm wraps around my waist, hauling me off my feet and into a waiting car.

"Let me go!" I scream, thrashing against my captor as he shoves me into the back seat.

"Shut up!" he snarls, speaking in heavily accented English before switching to rapid-fire Japanese.

He gets into the driver's seat and speeds into traffic. The man has his cell phone to his ear, his words foreign and unintelligible, but the menace in his voice is unmistakable.

My pulse races, and fear claws at my insides like a living thing.

I've gone from a mad woman to this maniac.

Who the hell is he?

What does he want with me?

"Please," I whisper, my voice trembling. "Please, release me. I'm Katarina Saunders, maybe you've heard of me? I'm in the band The Grinders. My children, my husband and my friends will be searching for me."

But my captor ignores me, continuing his conversation as if I am not there. I pull on the door handle, but it doesn't open. My only option for escape is through the man who's driving. He glances at me in the rearview mirror, ends his call, and lets his cell phone drop onto the passenger seat. The car accelerates through traffic, and he weaves in between cars. If I am going to attack him, I need to do it before he kills us both. He sharply turns the wheel, and we drive down a one-lane road. Instead of buildings, cars, and people, we are surrounded by trees, manicured gardens, and flowers.

The car comes to a sudden halt, jolting me back into the seat. My captor sits there in silence. I glance out the window, my heart pounding as I take in the vast estate before us. He's stopped in front of a house, its huge white pillars with gold accents towering above us.

"Where are we?" I choke out, fearing the answer.

He ignores me, steps out of the car, and opens my door with a jerk. I hesitate, then reluctantly exit the car, my legs shaky beneath me.

"Kat," a woman's voice calls out, and I look up to see a stunning Japanese woman standing on the steps of the opulent house. "Come inside," she says, her voice firm but gentle. "You must be tired."

"Who are you? What do you want with me?"

"Questions later," she replies, her eyes softening. "I am Kiyoko. First, you need to take care of yourself. Shower, change, and then we'll talk."

"I need to call my husband."

Kiyoko waves a hand in the air. "Patience," her tone is soothing yet authoritative. "You can call Dane soon. But first, you must clean up."

Whoever she is, she knows Dane even though I didn't mention his name. As much as I yearn to confront her and demand my freedom, I realize I'm left with no alternative.

Entering her lavish home, my captor closes the door behind us.

Kiyoko leads me along a hallway to a luxurious bathroom, complete with marble floors, gold fixtures, and an enormous tub that seems big enough to swim laps in. A set of fresh clothes lays folded neatly on the vanity, awaiting me.

"Take your time," Kiyoko instructs, closing the door behind her as she leaves.

Take my time? I think bitterly as I strip off my soiled clothes and step into the shower. *How can I take my time when Dane and the kids might be in danger?*

The hot water cascades over me, washing away the blood and grime. When I'm done, I do feel a tiny bit of relief before I dress quickly, pulling on the soft cotton shirt and jeans she provided. The door creaks open as I step out of the bathroom, revealing my captor standing guard in the hallway. His expression remains impassive, his hand gesturing for me to walk ahead of him.

"Where are we going?" I ask, my voice barely above a whisper.

"Living room," he replies curtly, not bothering to look at me as he points where I should go.

The living room is stunning, with floor-to-ceiling windows offering breathtaking ocean views. The moment I step into the living room, I see Kiyoko standing by one of the windows, her cell phone pressed against her ear. She spares me a glance before returning to the conversation.

"Ah yes, very good," she says smoothly. "May our organizations have a long, prosperous business arrangement." She faces me, a smile playing on her lips as she holds out the cell phone. "Your husband."

My heart leaps into my throat. I snatch the phone

from her hand, pressing it to my ear with trembling fingers. "Dane?" I breathe out, desperate for his voice and assurance he is okay.

"Kat, darlin', are you all right?" Dane's familiar, gravelly voice washes over me like a balm, and I feel tears prick at the corners of my eyes.

"Y-yeah," I stutter, collapsing onto a plush couch, the relief so overwhelming I can barely breathe. Great sobs escape me as I cling to the sound of his voice like a lifeline.

"Listen to me, Kat," he says, his voice tense but determined. "You're going to be okay. We're coming to get you. I'm here, darlin'. I'm here in Hawaii. Hang tight for now."

In the background, I can hear Sal's voice, deep and commanding, along with Tony's. They must be working together to find me, to bring me home. The thought brings a fresh wave of tears to my eyes.

"Okay," I whisper, wiping away the tears with the back of my hand.

"Stay strong, darlin'. Kiyoko is a… friend." He pauses. "I love you."

"I love you too," I choke out, the words barely audible through my sobs.

As the call ends, I looked up at Kiyoko, her dark eyes seemingly filled with genuine concern.

In that moment, I do not understand who this woman truly is, what her intentions are, or what she wants from my husband or me. All I know is

Dane says she's a friend, so I am safe at last.

I hand the phone back to Kiyoko. Her warm smile seems almost out of place in the opulent room. My heart pounds in my chest, a mix of relief and lingering fear.

"Can I get you anything?" Kiyoko asks, her voice is soft and gentle. "Tea, perhaps?"

"Uh, sure," I stammer, still trying to process this surreal situation.

As Kiyoko turns, she raises a hand toward a woman waiting in a doorway. The woman nods once and scurries away. I rub my wrists where the handcuff has dug into my skin. The pain is a stark reminder of what I have been through and how quickly things can change.

The woman returns, places a tray with a teapot and cups on the coffee table, bows at Kiyoko, and leaves the room.

"This will make you feel better." Kiyoko pours the tea and hands me a cup. "Here you go." She sits next to me on the couch. Her posture relaxed yet somehow regal.

"Thanks." I take a small sip. The warmth spreads through me, steadying my nerves ever so slightly.

"Your husband will be here soon," Kiyoko assures me, her eyes meeting mine. "You have nothing to worry about."

I do want to believe her, but as I look into her dark, enigmatic eyes, I cannot help but wonder who the hell this woman is and what her true intentions are.

CHAPTER
13

DANE

Salvatore's dark eyes are locked on the road ahead, steadfastness etched into every line of his face as he drives toward Kiyoko's home. Tony sits in the back, silent as the grave. The tension is thick enough to choke on as we are all lost in our own thoughts. For Tony, I'm sure he blames himself for Kat being taken in the first place.

"Never thought we'd be partnering up with the Obayashi Yakuza," I say. "But I guess you do what you have to do when family's involved."

Salvatore nods. "It's a dangerous game we're playing, Dane. But the benefits could be worth it. The Yakuza have power and connections we can't ignore."

"Let's hope they don't stab us in the back." My

grip tightens on the passenger door, and it creaks under the pressure.

The three of us ride through the gates of Kiyoko's estate. It is a sprawling compound surrounded by high walls and security cameras everywhere. As we pull up to the main house, the large wooden doors open to reveal a man with a shaved head wearing a suit.

His face is impassive as he greets us in broken English. "Welcome. Kiyoko-san is waiting for you."

"Lead the way," I growl, my heart pounding.

The man guides us through the opulent halls of Kiyoko's home, my boots echoing on the polished marble floor. My eyes dart from one closed door to the next, my heart pounding with each passing second. I can feel Salvatore and Tony's tension mirroring my own.

"Here," the man says, stopping before a set of double doors. He pushes them open, revealing a spacious room filled with plush furniture and ornate decorations.

"Kat," I whisper as my eyes lock onto her, sitting on a velvet couch, her face pale but her eyes defiant. The moment she sees me tears well in her vibrant green eyes, and she rushes into my arms.

"Thank God," I breathe out, wrapping her in a tight embrace, my relief morphing into white-hot anger at what she's been through. "I got you, baby."

"Hey," Salvatore interrupts gently, his voice low

and controlled. "Kiyoko, we can't thank you enough for finding Kat."

I hold Kat as if my life depends on it, my fingers digging into her waist, grounding myself with her presence. She clings to me just as desperately, her face buried in my chest.

Kiyoko gives us a curt nod. "It was the least I could do. Your wife is strong. She is made of steel."

"Damn right, she is." I can't help but think how close I'd come to losing her.

"Please, sit." Kiyoko gestures to the seats around a coffee table. We settle in, Kat never leaving my side, her hand gripping mine like a lifeline.

"Your partnership with the Obayashi Yakuza will benefit both parties," Kiyoko says, her gaze fixed on Salvatore. "But know that our loyalty comes at a price."

"Understood," Salvatore replies, his voice steady. "We won't forget what you've done for us."

"See that you don't." Kiyoko's eyes flick to mine, then back to Salvatore. "And remember, we will always be watching."

"Message received loud and clear," I say through gritted teeth, the weight of this new alliance settling in my gut like lead. But at least my woman is safe—it is all that matters right now.

Not wanting to waste any more time, as I know Kat will want to be back with our kids, I say, "I can't thank you enough for finding my wife. We'll honor any agreement and look forward to working with you in the future."

Kiyoko raises an eyebrow, clearly surprised by my genuine gratitude and love for Kat. "It's rare to see men of power love so deeply and act with such honor," she muses, her voice softening just a fraction.

"Kat means everything to me," I reply, tightening my grip on her hand. "I'd do anything for her and our children."

"Very well." Kiyoko nods. "Take your wife home, Dane Reynolds. We will be in touch."

"Thank you," I say once more before turning to Salvatore and Tony.

Sal holds up a hand. "We have things we need to discuss with Kiyoko. Take Kat home. We'll be there as soon as time allows."

Grateful I don't have to keep Kat here any longer than necessary, I stand, taking Kat with me. We walk through Kiyoko's home and out to the waiting car. I open the passenger door, and Kat climbs in. As we leave the lavish estate, Kat clings to my hand, silent tears streaming down her cheeks. My emotions threaten to consume me, but I force myself to focus on getting us home where she belongs.

As we continue driving, Kat's grip on my hand tightens, and I know she needs to let it all out—the fear, the pain, the uncertainty.

"Stop the car," she whispers, her voice trembling.

I pull over, concern for her almost overwhelming me.

"It was Stella..." she pauses, struggling to find the words. "She was... deranged, Dane. She murdered Gareth Goodman and Will Van Ryken."

"*Fuck.*"

Kat continues, her voice barely audible, "The room she kept me in was filthy, damp, and reeked of garbage. I tried to escape once, but she caught me, and for a while, I thought she wouldn't let me go."

"Jesus, Kat," I breathe out, pulling her closer to me. I cannot even begin to imagine the horror she has experienced.

"Stella thought she was protecting me, Dane. She tried to kill a man on a motorcycle, but she ended up dead instead."

"Protecting you?" I ask, anger flaring inside me at the twisted logic. "By kidnapping you?"

"I know it doesn't make sense, but in her twisted mind, she believed she was helping me."

"None of this should have ever happened, Kat." I hold her to my chest, determined to make sure nothing like this ever happens again. "I swear, I'll tighten security and won't let you go anywhere without me."

"Thank you, Dane," she whispers against my chest.

We sit here in silence for a moment, allowing the weight of everything to sink in before I start the car and continue driving home.

We have been driving for a while when Kat breaks the silence, her voice hesitant. "Dane, why did you send everyone away?"

I glance at her, not wanting to get into that conversation right now, but I know she deserves answers.

Sighing, I finally relent. "Kat, the Abruzzi Crime Family is no more," I say quietly. "It's now the Agostino Crime Family, and Salvatore is in charge."

Her eyes widen in understanding, but she doesn't say anything for a moment, letting the information sink in. Finally, she speaks up, "So either you or Sal... you took care of Don Abruzzi?"

I don't want to give her all the gruesome details, but she is smart enough to figure out what has happened without me having to spell it out for her. I nod, keeping my eyes on the road.

"Let's just say that Don Abruzzi won't be causing any more trouble for us or anyone else," I tell her, trying to keep my tone neutral.

"Okay." Kat rubs my arm. "I don't need to know everything, Dane. Just promise me we'll be safe. That our children will be safe."

"Darlin', I swear. I'll do whatever it takes to keep you all safe. Always."

The rest of the drive home is quiet, both of us lost

in our own thoughts. I can tell Kat is still processing everything that has happened. It's a lot to take in, but I hope, with time, things will start to feel normal again. All that matters is we are together and will do whatever it takes to protect our family.

As we pull up to our house, everyone is waiting outside. They have been through hell too, worrying about her.

Dave is the first to approach the car, his face a mix of relief and concern. He flings open the passenger door and holds out his arms. "Princess." Kat falls into his embrace as fresh tears stream down her cheeks. "Thank God you're safe."

"Thanks, Dave," Kat whispers, clinging to him as the older man has always been a father figure to her.

Truth, the lead singer of The Grinders, gently pries her away from him, and together, they lead Kat into the house.

The second she walks through the door, Jesse spots his mother and runs straight into her arms.

"Mommy!" he cries, tears running down his little face as he hugs her tightly.

Kristen follows suit, wrapping herself around her mother's waist.

Standing back, I watch my wife hold onto our children, their shared love and relief filling the room. It is a sight I will never forget and one that makes all the chaos and danger worth it in the end.

Emily and Luther enter the room, each carrying Blaze and Gunner.

Emily smiles at Kat, tears welling in her eyes. "Welcome home, Kat."

"Thank you, Em," Kat replies, her voice breaking as she looks around the room at all the people who love her.

My family is back together, safe and sound, and though I know there will be more challenges ahead—after all, life with the MC and the Agostino Crime Family will never be without challenges—I am confident we will face them head-on as long as we have each other.

"Welcome home, darlin'," I whisper to Kat, wrapping my arms around her and our children.

Tears stream down Kat's cheeks as she looks around at the people gathered in the room—all of them family.

"So, my princess of pop, what the hell happened?" asks Truth as his wife, Rosie, tucks into his side.

Kat shakes her head and looks down at her children. "Later."

I pull her into my arms, feeling her small frame shake with sobs. My throat tightens as I hold her there, whispering words of love and reassurance into her hair. One by one, the others join us, wrapping their arms around us in a group hug that speaks volumes about the bond we all share.

Savage Angels

"Family sticks together, no matter what," Truth states, his voice rough with unshed tears.

"Damn right," Dave agrees, his grip on Kat tightening for a moment before he lets go.

We stay like this for a few more minutes, lost in our shared relief and gratitude, until my cell phone buzzes in my pocket, breaking the spell. I glance at the screen, seeing an incoming call from Hilo Hellions.

With a sigh, I excuse myself from the embrace. "Club business, darlin'. I'll be right back."

Kat gives me a nod, her eyes still red-rimmed but filled with understanding. "Go ahead, Dane. We'll be here when you're done."

I leave the room, swiping my thumb across the screen to accept the call. "Dane. What's up?"

"Hey, man," the other MC president greets me. "Just checking in to see if our tip panned out. Did you find your wife?"

"Sort of," I reply, leaning against the wall. "Your info led us to a house, but nothing was there. Turns out the Obayashi Yakuza found her and took her in. She's safe now."

"Shit." Concern is evident in his voice. "You know what they say about dealing with the Yakuza, right? They only ever care about themselves. Make sure you watch your back, brother."

"Appreciate the heads-up," I say, my jaw tightening at the reminder of the potential

137

consequences for our club. "And thanks again for your help. We owe you one."

"Anytime, Dane. Just be careful, yeah?"

"Will do." I end the call and pocket my phone, taking a deep breath before returning to the room.

The dangers that still lay ahead can wait for now.

I want to focus on the fact we are all together once more, and are ready to face whatever comes our way.

Hours later, the house has fallen quiet, as everyone is asleep or in their rooms. I find myself lying next to Kat in our bed, feeling her breathing steady against my chest. She is here and safe, and it's all that matters.

"Hey." I brush a strand of hair from her face. "You okay?"

"Better now." Her eyes meet mine with a softness that makes me feel like I can breathe again.

"I'll never let anything happen to you again."

Our bodies seem to fit perfectly, two halves of a whole reunited. It feels like we are rediscovering each other, our fingers tracing familiar paths over skin and muscle, mapping out our love for one another.

"Touch me, Dane," Kat whispers, her voice barely audible, but her desire is clear. Her hands reach up to cradle my face, pulling me closer as our lips meet in a tender, passionate kiss.

Slowly, I begin to explore her body, my fingertips trailing fire along her skin, eliciting shivers and sighs as I touch her. Every caress is an affirmation of our love, a testament to the bond between us that nothing and no one can break.

"God, Kat, I need you," I admit, my voice thick with emotion as I position myself above her, ready to claim what is mine.

"Take me, Dane," she whispers, wrapping her legs around my waist, urging me on.

The tip of my cock slides into her wet entrance, joining our bodies together in a slow, deliberate rhythm. This isn't just sex but a healing, a redemption, and a promise of what we can face in this world together and come out united and stronger.

As our bodies move in sync, I whisper words of love and devotion in her ear, sealing each vow with a kiss. The world beyond our bedroom ceases to exist, leaving only us.

Kat closes her eyes, and I bend down, claiming her lips. "Give me your eyes, darlin'."

Through hooded lashes, she smiles at me. "Make me come, Dane."

I pull out of her and, in one fluid movement, flip Kat over. She knows what I want and goes up on all fours. My cock slides back into her as I wrap my arm around her tiny waist. Kat rocks back against me as my fingers apply pressure to her nub.

"Oh, yes," Kat cries as a shudder runs through her. *"Harder."*

"You need to help me."

Her hand goes between her legs, and I straighten up, gripping her hips, digging my nails into her soft flesh as she works herself, and I pound into her.

The noise of our bodies slapping against each other and our ragged breaths are the only sounds in the room.

"Faster," Kat begs.

Not wanting to disappoint her, I increase my speed, the full length of my cock sliding in and out as she grips the bed sheets with both hands. Kat's pussy contracts around my cock, and she arches her head back as her orgasm washes through her. It is only then I allow myself to come.

Kat's strength fades, causing her to crumple onto the bed as her arms give way. Slowly, I move in and out of her until I am spent, and then I pull out and drag her into my side as we regain a normal breathing rhythm.

She traces patterns on my chest, and I grab her

hand and kiss each finger before kissing her palm. "Mine."

"Always."

The morning sun filters through the curtains, casting its golden light across Kat's gorgeous body. She slept peacefully beside me, her face serene and untroubled.

"Morning," I greet as she stirs, her eyes fluttering open.

"Morning." Kat sleepily snuggles closer. "What time is it?"

"Doesn't matter," I say, kissing her forehead. "We've got all the time in the world."

I know there are still obstacles to overcome—my debt to Kiyoko, the Yakuza's involvement in our lives, and the ongoing threats against our club — but I also know we will face them head-on.

"Hey, darlin'," I say as we lay here, wrapped up in each other. "Do we have to get up and face the world?"

Kat sighs but nods. "Yeah, we do. Let's just take a moment, though."

Our bodies remain entwined, savoring that last

bit of serenity before reality comes crashing down once more.

We untangle ourselves from each other, and I follow her into the shower. My cock is again ready to take what is, and will always be, mine.

Kat giggles. "We should get dressed and get going."

Placing a hand on either side of her head, I nod. "We will, but I have something I need to do first."

"Need or want?"

Rubbing my nose against hers, I ask, "Does it matter?"

Kat giggles. "The kids, the band, everyone will want to see me."

Dropping to my knees, I look up at her as the water courses over my body. "They will. It's still early, the house is quiet, and I need you."

Kat smiles at me and places one of her legs over my shoulder. "Hungry?"

Smiling, I sink my tongue through her folds and find her tiny nub. Kat gasps as one hand goes to my head while the other grips onto the showerhead above. I suck and lap at her until she begs me to fuck her.

I rock back onto my heels and look up at her. "Tell me what you want."

"Fuck me."

Teasingly, I run a finger up her leg and slowly insert it inside her. "Like this?"

"No." She pants.

I move closer and suck on her nub while I move my finger in and out of her. "Like this?"

"Dane, baby, please don't make me beg."

"Tell me."

Kat slides her leg off my shoulder, pushes me back onto the cold tile, positions herself over my cock, and slams herself onto me, then moves her hips. "Like this."

Gripping her hips, I help her move back and forth as she stares down at me. I arch up, and she moves faster, riding me with wanton abandon.

Kat cries out as she comes, and I lose myself inside her as her pussy contracts around my cock.

A smile creeps across her face as she stares at me. "Mine."

"Always."

The house is buzzing with activity as everyone eats breakfast while Dave and Luther put more food on the table. The air is thick with tension but also with love and support.

"Does the public know what happened to me?" Kat asks.

Dave stops what he is doing and shakes his head. "No. As far as the public is concerned, you and The Grinders have disappeared, and no one knows where you are. No one knows about your ordeal, and they don't need to unless you want them to."

"What about the police?" Kat asks.

I shake my head. "The Yakuza are good at covering their tracks."

"Stella said we were around the corner from a police station. Surely, they know?"

Frowning, I say, "You were nowhere near a police station. She lied."

Kat shakes herself as though a shiver has gone through her. "I wonder what she had planned?"

"The main thing, my feisty friend, is that you're safe." Truth stabs a sausage from a platter in the middle of the table. "And thankfully, she is no more. Although, I am surprised about Will Van Ryken. How the hell did she even get close to him?"

Kat shakes her head. "She didn't really give me all the details, and I didn't ask."

"Should we tell someone?" asks Jamie.

"What's the point? He's dead, and telling isn't going to bring him back," I say.

Truth nods and sinks his teeth into the sausage. His flowery way of talking makes people think he's a pansy, but the man can fight, except if there's blood, then he's out like a light.

"How did we end up like this? What happened to

just playing music and enjoying life?" asks Blair.

"Life happens, babe," Kat replies. "But we'll get through this. We always do."

"All right, everyone. Let's pack it up," I say. "We've got a long trip back to Tourmaline."

Kat sighs and leans against me. "It'll be good to be home."

"Hey, Dane, you got a sec?" Jonas enters the room, his face serious.

Jasmin immediately stands and throws her arms around him. "Babe, where the fuck have you been?"

"Sugar, I've been working."

"I've missed you."

Judge grins. "Then spend some time in Tourmaline. Come home with us. You, me, and Noah can buy that house you're always talking about."

Jasmin screws up her face, and I think she's going to say no, but she smiles and nods. "Yeah, I'd like that."

Clearing my throat, I walk past them and out of the dining room to the other end of the house. Judge follows, his pace matching mine.

"What's up?" I ask, concern growing in the pit of my stomach as I look at him.

The smile drops from his lips. "Got some news from back home." He hands me a folded piece of paper. "You ain't gonna like it."

"Fuck." I take the note and scan its contents. My

blood runs cold as I read the words scribbled hastily across the page. "Shit's goin' down in Tourmaline."

"Seems like it," Judge agrees. "We gotta get back there, man. Sort this shit out."

"We were going to head home today, anyway, but I was hoping it would be peaceful." I crumple the paper in my fist. "The sooner we get back, the sooner we can deal with whatever the fuck's waiting for us."

"Yep." Judge gives me a firm nod before turning to go back to Jasmin.

"Everything okay?" Kat questions as I return to her side, her green eyes full of concern.

"Something's come up back home," I admit, not wanting to lie to her. "We need to head back to Tourmaline as soon as we're packed up."

"Is it serious?"

I hesitate for a moment, not wanting to worry her more than necessary. "Not sure yet, darlin'. But I promise, whatever it is, we'll handle it together, like always."

"Okay." She nods, her grip on my arm tightening. "Let's get going then."

"Everyone ready?" I call out as I buckle Kristen into her car seat while Kat ensures Jesse and the twins are safe.

With so many of us, we are in four separate cars. Shouts of affirmation answer me, and with one last glance at the beach house, I get in the car and drive toward the airport. Thankfully, Dave, the master at organizing travel, has ordered a plane trip home for all of us. It must have cost him a small fortune, but he said he didn't want to miss out on any more time with Kat and his grandchildren. I'm not complaining. I feel safer having all those who mean something to me close by.

When we touch down at the nearest airport to Tourmaline, Dave has again arranged for a bus to drive us all back home. Jesse and Kristen are tired and bickering at each other. Kat looks exhausted from looking after the twins, and all I want is some alone time with my wife and kids.

As we disembark, Kat with Blaze in her arms and me with Gunner, Sal moves to stand next to me.

"Do you need something, brother?" I ask.

"We will not be joining you in Tourmaline. I must return to Chicago. There are pressing matters that require my attention and cannot be postphoned."

"Does Emily know?"

Sal nods, but his lips turn down. "She is *not* happy with me. Unfortunately, I can't leave her with you. It's too dangerous right now."

"Sal, she's my sister. I'll protect her."

Sal smiles. "This is not a slight against you. I know you'd protect her, but after watching what you went through with Kat, I want to keep her and our children close. As the new head of the Abruzzi family, I have a target on my back."

We enter the airport, and what feels like a million flashes go off in our faces. The paparazzi have found us.

"Great," I groan. "And it's about time you called it the Agostino family."

Sal shrugs at my suggestion. "You have enough to deal with." Sal places a hand on my shoulder. "We will see you soon, and I'll be in touch over the Yakuza. Kiyoko might just solve all our problems."

Tony joins us. "Boss, I don't like this. Too many people."

Sal looks out over the mass of cameras and press, screaming for The Grinders to talk to them.

"They aren't interested in us, but yes, let's go home." Sal locks eyes with me. "Until next time, be safe, be well, and take care of yourselves."

"You too, brother."

He lightly touches Gunner's head and then moves toward Emily, who gives me a tired wave as Sal whisks her off in search of another flight to Chicago.

"Are they leaving?" asks Kat.

"Sal needs to get back... work."

Kat repositions Blaze in her arms and then puts on a fake smile for the press. "Lucky Sal. You ready for this?"

"No."

Kat laughs. "The joys of being married to a rock star."

"Oh, darlin', there are many joys, but the press, thinking they own you, isn't one of them."

She nods, but we both know the press will want their pound of flesh, so we move toward the waiting crowd with the rest of her band. Dave is already barking orders at them, reminding them we have babies and if they should get jostled in any way, he will sue all of them.

CHAPTER 14

SALVATORE

The whispers in the dark corners of the city echo with the news of Don Abruzzi's demise. Like a vengeful wildfire, it spreads and solidifies my place as the new head of the Abruzzi Crime Family. I can feel the weight of their stares on my back, sharp like the wire that ended the Don's reign.

My mind wanders back to the events that led me here—the late nights, the deals gone wrong, the blood staining my hands. The sacrifices I made for this goddamn family weigh heavily on my soul, and the faces of those I lost haunt my dreams.

The time has come to call a meeting of the families. I want to address any concerns head-on to show them I am every bit as strong and capable as Don Abruzzi had been. I stand at the head of the long, polished table, feeling a renewed sense of purpose course through my veins. This is my moment, my chance to prove my worth.

"Listen up," I say, my voice echoing through the dimly lit room. "I know some of you have doubts about me taking over. I get it. But I am not here to replace Don Abruzzi. I'm here to carry on his legacy, to forge my own path forward, and to bring us kicking and screaming into this century, whether you like it or not."

Tarso Lombardi, the grizzled old head of his family, narrows his eyes at me from across the table. "You think you got what it takes to rule us?" he growls, his voice thick with skepticism.

"Look," I reply, meeting his gaze without flinching. "I am not going to apologize for who I am or where I come from. I'm bringing something new to the table that's going to help us expand into new markets and territories." Their curiosity is piqued, but I know I have to drive the point home.

The room goes deathly silent as I open the door and let her enter. She walks in with an air of confidence that makes even the most hardened man in the room take notice. The fact she is a woman does not matter, her very presence demands respect.

"Allow me to introduce you to Kiyoko of the Obayashi Yakuza."

"Yakuza?" Tarso scoffs, his face twisted in

disbelief. "You bringin' outsiders into our organization?"

"Times are changing, Tarso," I reply, my voice steady and calm. "And if we don't change with them, we're going to be left behind." I can see the uncertainty in their eyes, but I hold firm. This is the future, whether they like it or not.

"Besides," I add, a sly grin spreading across my lips. "I think you'll find that Kiyoko here is more than capable of holding her own."

The tension in the room is thicker than a fog on the Hudson. Tarso, his face red with anger, slams his hand down on the table, making glasses shudder.

"Women and outsiders don't sit at our table!" he bellows.

Kiyoko's smile is like a shark surveying its prey. I can see her calculating, ready to strike. She leans back in her chair, not a hint of fear in her eyes.

"Tell me, Tarso," she says sweetly. "How are your deals with the gangs in Atlanta going?"

His face goes from red to crimson as he clenches his teeth, admitting, "We're in an all-out war."

"Such a shame," Kiyoko replies, her voice dripping with mock sympathy. "You know, with a single phone call, I can end your troubles." Her eyes lock onto his, and I feel a chill run down my spine.

Is this what it takes to survive in the new world? To cut through the bullshit and lay it all out on the table? To show these old-timers we aren't fucking around?

As Kiyoko stares down Tarso, I feel a shift in the room. Every eye is on her, waiting to see if she will follow through on her promise. The silence is deafening.

"Okay," Tarso says, his voice dripping with skepticism. "If you can actually accomplish this... if you can end my troubles in Atlanta with a single phone call, I'll yield. I won't speak another word against Salvatore Agostino."

"Very well," Kiyoko replies, her smile never faltering. She pulls out her cell phone and dials a number, speaking briefly in Japanese before hanging up. "Done," she announces, her icy gaze still fixed on Tarso.

I cannot help but be impressed by her boldness. She has walked into a lion's den, unafraid and undeterred. This is the kind of ally we need— someone who will not back down when shit gets real.

I sit back in my chair, watching the exchange between Tarso and Kiyoko. I have no idea what she has done, but the fact she is not showing an ounce of fear or emotion in front of these hardened men is impressive as hell.

"Really?" Tarso asks, his voice betraying a hint of incredulity. "Just like that?"

"Efficiency is one of our strong suits," Kiyoko

replies coolly. Her words are measured and confident. "You'll see soon enough."

"Remember this day, gentlemen," I say, my voice firm. "This is the dawn of a new era. You can either get on board or get the hell out of our way."

And as I look around the room, I see that some are ready to embrace the change while others cling to their outdated ways.

But it does not matter.

The future is coming.

The tension in the room is palpable. The other men at the table are on edge, unsure about how to react to the woman who has waltzed into their world and thrown everything off balance. But beneath the tension, I sense something else—a grudging respect. Kiyoko has balls, and even the most stubborn of these guys are starting to acknowledge that.

"Let's not forget why we're here," I say, addressing the table. My voice is steady and authoritative. "We're all in this together. We need to work as one if we're going to survive in this cutthroat world."

My words seem to have an effect as the atmosphere in the room shifts ever so slightly. Some of the men nod, while others exchange wary glances. They are beginning to understand that they need to adapt or get left behind.

"Trust me," I add, my gaze sweeping over the

faces of the men who have been my brothers-in-arms for years. "This alliance with the Obayashi will be good for all of us."

As the meeting progresses, I can feel the tide turning in my favor. It is clear that some of the families still have their reservations, but I know actions speak louder than words. And with Kiyoko by my side, there is no doubt in my mind we will show them all how far we are willing to go to protect our interests.

As we wrap up the meeting, I cannot help but feel a strange mixture of excitement and trepidation. We are entering uncharted territory, forging a new path in a constantly evolving world.

A knock sounds on the door, and the room goes silent. One of Lombardi's crew members slinks in, looking like a rat caught in a trap. He leans in close to Tarso, whispering something that makes the man's eyes widen as though he has seen a ghost.

"Excuse the interruption," Tarso mutters, his face pale.

As the man scurries out, I glance at Kiyoko, who has an amused smile dancing on her lips. "Well?" she asks, her voice dripping with confidence. "Are you satisfied, Tarso?"

Tarso hesitates for a moment before nodding stiffly. "I will accept Salvatore as the new head of the *Agostino* Crime Family."

It is not lost on me or anyone else at the table

that Tarso Lombardi called us the Agostino Crime Family instead of the Abruzzi Crime Family.

"All right then." I stand, feeling the weight of their gazes on me. "Listen up because I am *not* going to say this twice. The Obayashi is the first step in our evolution. Be prepared for more."

"Are you suggesting we let outsiders run our business?" someone scoffs from the table.

"No. But we will be opening our ranks to new blood, regardless of their affiliations. You will all show respect to the Savage Angels. I will consult some or all of you on various matters, but the final decision will be made by me. If you can't bend to this new direction, you're on your own. And trust me, plenty of outsiders are ready to pick you apart and take your place."

The room goes quiet, the tension thick enough to cut with a knife. But I do not flinch. This is my show now, and they must accept it.

"Good," I say, holding their gazes until, one by one, they look away. "Now get the hell outta here and start making some changes."

They file out of the room, leaving me alone with Kiyoko. I feel the gravity of what has happened, and a part of me cannot help but wonder if I have bitten off more than I can chew.

Kiyoko bursts into laughter, and her dark eyes twinkle. "You should have seen their faces, Salvatore! Priceless!"

"All right, all right," I say, trying to keep my laughter in check. "What did you do, Kiyoko? Really?"

She looks at me like I am a naïve kid, smirking. "I simply eliminated the threat to our organization," she says matter-of-factly.

"Eliminated?" My eyebrows shoot up. "All of them?"

"Of course. It's how we do things," she replies, her tone casual, as if it were nothing more than a day's work. "Salvatore, you made the right decision. The world doesn't wait for those who cling to the past. Bringing in the Obayashis is smart, and together we are stronger."

I shake my head, not quite able to wrap my mind around it. It's clear these Japanese have a different way of doing business. But maybe it is something that can serve us well—for now, anyway.

"Listen, Kiyoko," I say, leaning against the table. "We have to make sure we're on the same page here. We're partners, but this is still my family we're talking about, and I will not let anyone walk all over us."

"Relax, Salvatore." She places a hand on my shoulder. "I know my place. And I respect your loyalty to your men. But remember, we're all in this together. We must be prepared to do whatever it takes to protect our interests, even if it means getting our hands dirty."

"Dirty is one thing." I run a hand through my hair. "This shit feels downright filthy."

The Abruzzi Crime Family has always had a heavy hand when it comes to dealing with those who would oppose us.

But wiping out an entire gang?

This is not something we have ever done.

Individuals?

Yes.

To make a point, we leave some behind alive as a warning so none will ever dare to try again. But the Yakuza destroy all who oppose them, not just the head of the snake, they take the whole snake pit.

"Filthy or not, it's the world we live in," Kiyoko counters. "You wanted change, didn't you? This is what it looks like."

I sigh, knowing she is right. We are knee-deep in this now, and there is no turning back. If we were going to thrive, then maybe it is time to embrace the unfamiliar, even if it scares the shit out of me.

"All right." I nod. "But remember, Kiyoko, I'm watching you. And I expect you to watch my back too."

"Of course, Salvatore... that's what partners are for, isn't it?"

"Damn right." I fix her with a stare. "Now, let's get the hell out of here and start making some waves."

Kiyoko stands, nods at me out of respect, and

leaves the room. The heavy door slams shut, echoing through the now-empty room. I stare at the long table, littered with the remnants of what we have just hashed out. The air is thick with power shifts and new beginnings.

I leave the meeting room with an overwhelming need to see my wife and children.

Lorenzo waits for me, leaning against my car. He opens the back door, and I climb in. The windows are tinted, so you can't see inside the vehicle. I sit open-legged on the seat and hit the button so the interior glass slides down, and I can talk to Lorenzo. He already has the car started and gets ready to drive.

"Where to?"

"Home."

"You okay, Sal?"

"The Yakuza wiped out a gang in Atlanta to prove they are on our side."

He looks at me in the rearview mirror. "Are you fucking kidding me?"

"No." I loosen my tie. "Keep an eye on them. As much as I want to trust them, we should be cautious. Do we have anyone on the inside of their organization?"

Lorenzo smirks. "Yes."

"Make sure they keep us informed."

He stops the car and moves to open his door so he can open mine.

"Stay." Lorenzo twists to face me. "I might be Don, but I can still open my own fucking door. Do you want to come in? Have a bite to eat?"

"No, boss. I've got a date."

Chuckling, I ask, "A date... date. Or a paid date?"

Lorenzo scoffs. "Boss? You think so little of me." He shakes his head. "A date. You'd like her. She's a good Catholic girl."

I open my door. "Are you thinking of settling down?"

He grins. "Never said that."

With a two-fingered wave, I step out into the night. The air is cold against my face as I walk to the front door and unlock it. All I want is to put this entire day behind me.

"Sal?" Emily calls from the kitchen. "Is that you?"

"Yeah, amare," I call back, hanging my coat on the rack. "It's me."

"Did everything go okay at the meeting?" she asks, concern etching her beautiful face.

I can tell she has been worried sick about me. Hell, I have been worried sick about me too.

"More or less." I pour myself a glass of red wine before I sit at the kitchen island. "But there's something I have to do before I can even think about relaxing." I pull out my cell phone.

"Who're you calling?"

"Your brother," I reply, taking a deep breath as I wait for him to pick up.

"Sal?" Dane's voice sounds gruff.

"Remember the deal we made with Kiyoko and the Yakuza?" I ask. "Well, they got themselves a seat at the table. They're going to be working alongside us."

"How the hell did you manage to make that happen?" Dane sounds surprised.

"Long story." I rub a hand over my face. "But it's done now. I just want to say..." I pause, looking over at Emily, who is watching me, "... I'm grateful to you for trusting me through all this shit. We're going to be okay, Dane. Kat's safe, and so are the rest of us."

"Damn right, we are," Dane's voice is steady and determined. "We're family, love and loyalty."

"True. Take care, brother. I'll see you soon."

"See you soon," he repeats before hanging up.

As I set the phone down, I feel Emily's arms wrap around me from behind, her warmth chasing away some of the chill that's settled in my bones. This is where I belong, with my family and against whatever the world throws at us.

"Let's eat." Emily kisses my neck. "And then we can talk about everything that happened today."

"Sounds good, amare." I put my hands over hers, keeping her close. "What did you cook?"

"I wasn't sure how late you'd be, so I cooked something that would keep... lasagna."

Twisting on the seat, I pull her around so I can stare into her eyes. "My favorite."

"You say that about everything I cook."

Kissing her lips lightly, I reply, "Well, you cook everything well."

Emily smiles. It reaches her eyes, and she looks more beautiful to me than the day we first met. And knowing she cooked something that would keep, no matter what time I arrived home, speaks to the kind of woman she is. No fancy dinners but hearty ones to feed her family and let us know we are loved.

"Where are the children?"

"In bed and hopefully asleep, but I think Vincent is waiting up for you."

"Should I go up?"

Emily shakes her head. "No. This is our time. You can check on him later. Tony was reading to him and hasn't come down yet."

Laughing, I say, "Do you think he's fallen asleep again?"

Emily moves away from me and opens the oven. "Definitely." She puts the bubbling lasagna on the kitchen counter. "And the new guy made himself known to me and the children." Emily tilts her head to the side. "Sal, that makes six new bodyguards. Is it really necessary?"

"What happened to Kat will *never* happen to you."

She nods. "You know what's best."

Sipping my wine, I watch as she bustles around the kitchen, serving the lasagna and taking a salad out of the refrigerator.

"Are you happy?"

Emily pulls out a stool and sits next to me. "Yes. Are you?"

"Yes." I put a hand on her knee.

"But I must confess, I'd be happier if you poured me a glass of red too."

Grinning, I lean in and kiss her. "Your wish is my command."

CHAPTER 15

DANE

The wind roars in my ears as I lead Dirt and Kade down the freeway, Chicago's skyline looming ahead. We are gritty from the miles we have put behind us, but goddamn, it feels good to ride like this again. The trip with these two men has been bittersweet. One of them doesn't know he will not be returning with us. This decision was mine alone, but the other patched-in members of the Tourmaline chapter agreed with me, and we voted on it. How he reacts, no one knows.

"Salvatore's office should be just up ahead," I shout over the roar of our Harleys, nodding toward a red-brick two-story building. It blends in with the shops on either side of it. No one would know the leader of the Agostino family works from here. As we pull into the parking lot beside it, I cannot help but smile at the sight of us—dirty, grimy bikers surrounded by what feels like mom-and-pop businesses and clean streets. We definitely stand out, but it's just how we like it.

"Let's get this done, boys," I say, killing the engine and swinging my leg over the bike.

We walk the short distance to Salvatore's building and pull on the old steel door. It swings open with a loud creak to reveal him standing there, hands clasped behind his back, his dark eyes sizing us up.

"Sal," I greet him warmly, pulling him into a tight embrace. "Thanks for meeting with us."

"Of course, Dane," he replies, stepping aside to let us in. "I've always got time for my brother-in-law."

We follow him through the foyer, through another door, and into a large space with one of the biggest oak tables I have ever seen. The top is so polished you can see your reflection in it. Most of the walls have plaster on them, but here and there, the red brick shows through, giving it an almost homey feel. Sal sits at the head of the table and gestures for us to sit in the deep leather chairs flanking the table. Sal has been a rock through the nightmare of Kat's kidnapping, and I need him to know how much his support means to me.

"Sal, I have to say, you've really come through for

me and my family during that whole shitstorm," I begin, holding his gaze steadily. "You've had our backs, and I want you to know I'll never forget it."

"Family's everything, Dane," he replies seriously. "We do what we have to do for the ones we love."

"Damn straight," I agree, feeling a surge of gratitude for this man who is both my friend and my family.

"Sal, I have important news to tell you." I glance at my men. "We've got some changes happening in the Tourmaline chapter. Dirt's going step down as sergeant-at-arms."

Salvatore raises an eyebrow in surprise.

Dirt stands. "What the fuck?"

Rising from my chair, I face one of my oldest friends. "You haven't been happy since Lore came back on the scene. Dirt, my brother, it's time for you to move on. You know it, I know it, so I made the decision for you."

"There has to be a vote." Dirt frowns.

"There was one," I state.

"You can't fucking kick me out."

Reaching out, I lay a hand on his shoulder. "You're not out. No one wants you gone, but you've been a miserable bastard since you got back."

Kade barks out a laugh, and Dirt glares at him.

"Dane's right, you haven't been happy." Kade holds up his hands in mock surrender.

"Who's taking his place?" asks Sal.

"Kade," I answer, nodding toward the younger man. "He's got the skills and has earned the brothers' respect. I'm confident he'll do us proud."

"Congratulations, Kade." Salvatore gives him a chin lift. "I look forward to seeing how you help shape the future of the Savage Angels MC."

"Thanks, Sal," Kade replies.

Dirt looks from me to Kade, his expression carefully guarded after his earlier surprise. He runs a hand through his dirty blond hair.

"It's true. I love the club and all, but Lore... she's my world now. I can't keep putting her through hell because of my choices." Dirt's voice is thick with emotion.

I nod, understanding all too well what it feels like to have someone you love more than anything else in the world. "That's why you won't be coming home with us, Dirt. The patched-in members already voted Kade in as the new sergeant-at-arms for Tourmaline."

Dirt stares at me, trying to process what I am saying. He blinks a few times, clearly choked up, but then he gives me a sad smile. "Been one hell of a ride, hasn't it, Dane?" His voice cracks slightly.

"Damn right, it has. You've stood by me through thick and thin, brother. You're family, and I trust you with my life. But I also want you to be happy, and if that means leaving Tourmaline to be with Lore, then you have my blessing."

Kade stands and extends his hand to Dirt. "I've always admired you, man," he tells him sincerely. "You're leaving huge shoes to fill, and I'll do my damnedest to make you proud."

Dirt hesitates for a moment, still coming to terms with the enormity of it all, before accepting Kade's outstretched hand and shaking it firmly.

"Make sure you keep these boys in line," he says gruffly, giving Kade a nod of respect.

"You're still in. I expect you to keep in touch and check in from time to time."

I know this moment marks the end of an era, but it is also the beginning of something new. It is time for us to forge our own paths, to protect what matters most to us, no matter where those paths may lead.

In that moment, I know that no matter the obstacles we face, we will rise above them. We'll strengthen our bonds, protect our loved ones, and carve out our place in the world. And as long as we have each other, nothing can stand in our way.

"Here's to new beginnings," I say, raising an imaginary glass. "And to the future of our families and organizations."

"Cheers," Salvatore agrees, a determined glint in his eyes.

"Cheers," Kade echoes, his voice filled with promise.

Hours later, I'm standing on the sidewalk with Dirt and Kade. Dirt rips off his sergeant-at-arm's patch and hands it to Kade. With Dirt's departure final, I turned my attention to Salvatore, who's been standing off to the side, patiently waiting for our conversation to wrap up. We need to discuss our plans to protect our families and organizations from any future threats that might come our way. It's time to make sure none of us will ever be caught off guard again.

"This isn't goodbye," I state as Dirt grips my hand in a firm shake.

"I know."

"I meant it when I said you will need to check in. Don't make me come to Willowbrook Falls. Lore would fucking hate it."

Dirt barks out a laugh and nods. "Yeah, she would." He shuffles from foot to foot. Dirt has never been one for public displays of affection. "Well, I'll be off then."

Pulling him in for a hug, I slap his back firmly several times. "Don't be a stranger."

Dirt nods, steps out of my embrace, shakes hands with Kade, and walks to his bike. He climbs on, grins at us, and kick starts his machine.

"May the road rise to meet you, the wind always be at your back, the warm sun's rays fall upon your home, and the land of a friend always be near." Dirt pulls away, and we watch him until he disappears around the corner.

"Is Dirt Irish?" asks Kade.

"On his mother's side."

Salvatore steps out of his office and gives me a chin lift. "Are you two hungry? I can order takeout while we talk."

"I could eat." I glance at Kade, who nods.

"I'll go." Kade points across the street to a burger place. "Is it any good?"

Sal shrugs. "No idea. I guess we'll find out."

Kade grins and walks away then turns around. "One or two?"

"Two and fries and a Coke."

"Sal?"

"I'll have the same."

Sal opens the door to his building, and I walk back through to the long table, where we resume our seats.

"Sal, we need to talk about how we're going to keep our people safe going forward."

He nods solemnly. "Agreed. We can't afford any more slipups, Dane. What happened to Kat… it can't happen again."

"Damn right," I growl. "So, how do we do this?

How do we make sure nobody messes with our families or our organizations?"

Salvatore thinks for a moment, then says, "We need to tighten security around our homes and businesses. I've already increased the number of bodyguards in and around mine, and you might not have noticed them, but there are five men outside keeping an eye on me. No one gets in here without an invite."

"We did." I smirk.

"You had an invitation." Sal shakes his head and says, "We need to install top-of-the-line surveillance systems and ensure we've got eyes on every exit and entrance."

"Good plan," I agree. "And we should have regular check-ins between our clubs and your organization. If something goes down, everyone needs to know about it ASAP."

"Absolutely. I also think we need to be more proactive in gathering intel. Tap into the criminal underworld, cultivate informants, and stay one step ahead of our enemies."

"Smart," I reply, nodding. "We gotta be like fucking ghosts, man. Unseen and unheard until it's too late for anyone who tries to cross us."

As we continue to discuss our strategies, I cannot help but reflect on everything we have been through together. The sacrifices we have made, the pain we have endured—it has all taken a toll on us, both emotionally and physically.

"Y'know, Sal..." I say quietly. "We've been through some real shit together. We've lost people we cared about, and we've done things that'll haunt us for the rest of our lives."

"I know, Dane. But we did what we had to do to protect our families and our people. And we'll keep doing it, no matter what it takes."

"We'll face whatever comes our way, side by side, like brothers."

"Like brothers," he repeats.

Kade knocks on the door and walks in with a couple of bags of food.

"They were quick and did my order before anyone else's."

Sal grins. "They must have seen you talking to me."

"You mean it wasn't my good looks?" Kade teases as he hands each of us our food and drinks.

Sal chuckles, and we begin to eat.

"It's good." I put a fry in my mouth. "We'll eat, then be on our way."

"You're not staying?" asks Sal.

"No. Kade here has a woman who'll skin me alive if I keep him away too long."

Kade shakes his head. "I'd love to disagree with you, but yeah, Destiny likes me to stay close to home."

Sal waves a hand in the air. "Nothing wrong with

having a woman who wants to keep you close. And if that woman is beautiful?" Kade nods. "Then all the better."

Laughing, I say. "Yeah, she's beautiful, smart, and, for some reason, picked you."

Kade frowns. "Yeah. I often wonder if it hadn't been for—"

"Don't," I cut him off. "Destiny didn't pick you because of that piece of shit."

Kade nods and goes back to his burger. Sal looks at me quizzically, but I keep eating. There's no sense in rehashing the past. Destiny is a strong woman, and she didn't pick Kade as a second prize after that bastard raped her. It's obvious to all who know them that they are meant for each other.

"All right, Sal," I say, rubbing my hands together. "Time to talk about the future. We've been through hell and back, and now we need to focus on building our organizations back up, stronger than before."

Salvatore leans back in his chair, stroking his chin thoughtfully. "You're right, Dane. We need to expand our businesses and make sure we're covering all bases. Like real estate, for example. There's plenty of potential there."

"Definitely. And with how things are going these days, we can't forget about the online world either. Gambling, retail outlets... shit, even sex toys." I let out a rough laugh.

"Sex toys?" Salvatore raises an eyebrow,

chuckling. "Well, as long as it brings in the cash, right?"

"Damn straight," I say. "People will always want to get off one way or another. Might as well profit from it."

"Spoken like a true businessman, my friend. But seriously, we need to be smart about this. Keep our noses clean, stay ahead of the game."

"True that." I nod.

As we continue discussing our plans, I feel a renewed sense of purpose coursing through my veins. Yeah, we have faced some dark times but came out the other side ready to take on whatever life throws at us.

"Here's to the future, Sal. May it be filled with prosperity, power, and a shitload of sex toys."

"Cheers to that," Salvatore laughs. "Together, we'll face whatever challenges come our way."

And with that, our conversation draws to a close.

We have a long road ahead of us, but we are ready to face it head-on, united in our determination to protect what is ours and build a better future for our families and organizations.

We head through the building and out to where our bikes are waiting. Kade and I mount them, the roar of the engines shattering the quiet of the streets when we rev them to life. With a nod of understanding between us, Kade falls in behind me as we pull out of the parking lot and onto the open road, bound for Tourmaline.

As the wind whips through my hair and the miles fly by beneath our wheels, I cannot help but feel a sense of hope for the future. With renewed dedication and unbreakable bonds, we will forge ahead into a brighter future.

And as the road stretches out before me, leading back to Kat and the home we have built together, I know that whatever challenges come next, we will face them head-on.

CHAPTER
16

DIRT

As I roll into Willowbank Falls, the deep rumble of my Harley echoes through the empty streets. There's nothing like the throaty growl of a hog to announce your presence. The wind tugs at my hair, and the scar on my temple tingles with anticipation. I can't wait to see Lore's beautiful face again. It feels like a lifetime since I last held her in my arms.

The familiar sign of Rock Anthem Ale House comes into view, and my heart pounds at the thought of the woman inside. I park my bike out front and take a moment to steel myself before striding in, boots thudding against the hardwood floor.

"Welcome to the Rock Anthem—" Lore breaks off midgreeting, her gray eyes sparkling with surprise and joy. A smile spreads across her face, warm as the summer sun, and my chest tightens at the sight of her.

"Hey, baby," I say, my voice husky from the road as she bounds toward me.

She leaps into my arms, legs wrapped around my waist and arms encircling my neck. I wince involuntarily as her weight settles on my injured shoulder, and she instantly pulls back, concern etched on her face.

"Did I hurt you?" she asks, brows furrowed with worry.

"Ah, it's nothin', babe." But she is not buying it.

She studies me for a moment, then her fingers deftly pull down the collar of my T-shirt, revealing the healing bullet wound. "Jesus, Dirt! What the hell happened?"

I shrug, trying to play it off like it is not a big deal. "Took a hit for Dane. Part of the job, you know?"

"Part of the job? You could have been killed!" Lore's voice trembles and I can see the fear in her eyes.

"Hey, hey," I soothe, cupping her face in my hands. "I'm here, aren't I? Still breathing, still standing. That's what matters."

But she does not look convinced. And I know there is no easy way to tell her that this is par for the course in my world, but it is a world I'll gladly leave behind if it means keeping her by my side.

Lore climbs out of my arms and backs away from me. I see the wheels turning in her head. She's trying to make sense of it all, but I need her to know I am still here for her.

"Hey, babe," I say, holding up my hands in mock surrender. "Look, my sergeant-at-arms patch is gone." I point to the spot on my cut where the patch used to be. "I'm still in the club, but I'm not calling the shots anymore." I shrug. "I'm only a soldier now, one of many." Taking a step toward her, I continue, "If you'll have me, I'd like to stay. With you."

Her eyes search mine as if she is weighing the odds. I have to make sure she knows how much she means to me.

"Lore, I love you. Hell, I even love your grumpy-ass cat, Cosmo." A smile tugs at her lips, and I know I've got her. "You mean everything to me. I'd give up anything for you. You gotta know that."

Laughter bubbles up from her throat, and it's like music to my ears. "Dirt, you always knew how to make me laugh." Her gaze softens, and I can feel the tension ebbing away between us. She grabs a dishcloth from behind the bar and tosses it my way. "You remember how to clean a glass and serve a beer, right?"

"Like ridin' a bike, babe." I grin, catching the cloth with ease.

My heart swells as I step behind the bar, ready to do whatever it takes to keep this woman in my life.

The future doesn't look so dark anymore, and I know we will face it together.

I am all smiles as I stride behind the bar, feeling like I've been handed a second chance at life. The clink of glasses and Lore's laughter fill the air, mixing with the hum of conversation from our customers. It is a symphony that speaks to my soul, letting me know I'm right where I belong.

"Hey Dirt, grab me another round, will ya?" a familiar voice calls out from the end of the bar. I nod, my fingers dancing over the taps with practiced ease, pouring the perfect pint for an old friend.

"Comin' right up, brother," I say, sliding the frosty glass down to him. He raises it in salute, and I cannot help but return the gesture. It might not be the same as riding side by side, but this camaraderie still means something to me.

As the night wears on, I watch Lore work her magic with the patrons, her smile brightening the room like a damn sunbeam. My heart swells with love for this woman, who has made every sacrifice worth it.

"Ready to call it a night, babe?" she asks, leaning against the bar, sweat glistening on her forehead.

"Whenever you are," I reply, wiping down the last of the sticky countertops. We lock up together, and as we head toward her office, I know it's time to leave one part of my life behind.

My cut feels heavy in my hands, the weight of all those years pressing down on me. But I am not looking back now. I hang it up in her office, my eyes lingering on the empty space where my sergeant-at-arms patch used to be. A symbol of the man I was and the man I am going to be.

"Ready?" Lore asks, her hand reaching out to me. I take it without hesitation, our fingers entwining like the roots of a tree, strong and unbreakable.

"Ready for anything, babe," I say, my voice steady with conviction. We step out into the cool night air, the moon casting a silver glow over the quiet streets of Willowbank Falls. The future stretches before us like an open road, filled with possibilities and the promise of brighter days.

We walk away from Rock Anthem Ale House, arms wrapped around each other, and I lead her to my Harley. Deep in my bones, I know that together, we can conquer whatever life throws our way.

CHAPTER 17

DANE

The streets of Tourmaline are quiet this early in the morning. I am making my way to Betty's Café for breakfast, the sun beating down on my back. Life is good. The club is doing well, and Kat is at home with our children. Motherhood suits her. I'm lost in my thoughts when a shot rings out, and the world around me shatters.

"Shit!" I yell, hitting the pavement behind a parked car. Glass from Betty's Café showers down like deadly rain, and my heart races like a damn jackhammer.

This is not supposed to happen here.

Not in our town.

Screams sound from inside the café and cut through the air like a hot knife. I peer over the hood of the car, trying to make sense of what the fuck just happened.

"Prez!" I hear Kade yell as he and other MC members come running toward me. "You okay?"

"Fine," I grunt, my eyes locked on the busted window of Betty's Café. More shots slam into the building, sending dust and debris flying. Whoever is behind this is sending a clear message—they want me fucking dead, and they do not care who gets caught in the damn crossfire.

"Stay down, Prez!" Kade shouts.

But I can't just sit here while my people are in danger. Pushing myself to my feet, I move toward the open doorway of the café. A screech of tires causes me to turn to a car speeding down Main Street.

Who the fuck would have the balls to try this shit?

Kade stumbles through the open doorway, gun in his hand. "Prez!"

Holding up a hand, I say, "I'm fine. I'm not hit."

The metallic tang of blood fills my nostrils, making my stomach churn. Thea rises from behind the counter, her hands covered in blood. She looks at me and screams, but as if she cannot help it, her eyes lock onto something I can't see.

In one fluid movement, I leap over the counter. The lifeless body of Howie is sprawled out on the old linoleum floor. He is face up with a gruesome bullet hole between his eyes. Blood pools around him, staining the world red. It is a fucked-up sight. Howie is a young man in his prime, his life cut short by some fucker trying to kill me.

Howie was always good to Kat and me. His laughter and easy-going nature made everyone feel welcome. The thought of never seeing his friendly smile again twists my gut into knots.

Thea is holding her hands up, her mouth opening and closing as though trying to speak, but the words won't come. I move toward her, blocking her view of Howie's lifeless body.

"Kade, take her out of here," I order. "Don't let anyone else in. The sheriff is going to have a fit as it is."

"Got it, Prez." He gently but firmly pulls Thea away from the carnage. "Come on, Thea, let's get you outside."

"Call Renny." Kade nods at me as he takes her outside.

Thea is Renny's old lady, and they have a son together.

Jonas, my VP, looks at me through the shattered window of the café. "What happened?"

"Drive-by," I growl. My veins pulse with rage, demanding retribution. "Get your fucking asses on your bikes and track down that car heading out of town. Make sure they don't get far."

"On it," Jonas says as he jogs back toward the compound.

"Kade, go with Jonas."

"I'm not going to leave you here alone. Who knows if they'll come back for another round?"

"They're gone. I trust you and Jonas to find them. I know neither of you will let me down."

Kade hesitates for a moment, looking torn, but then jogs after Jonas.

He yells, "You better stay put then, Prez. Don't do anything stupid."

"Go," I urge him, my voice low and deadly. "And make them pay."

Thea is shaking uncontrollably, so I pull her into my chest. Her blood-stained hands clutch onto my white T-shirt as she sobs.

The sirens from the local law sound down Main Street as their flashing lights pull up in front of Betty's Café. Sheriff Carlos Morales steps out of one of the vehicles and stalks toward me. Although his expression is controlled, I know he'll be angry at the turn of events.

"Have you sent for Renny?" Carlos asks, his tone firm but not unkind.

Still holding onto Thea, I nod. Carlos enters the café, eyes scanning the carnage as he walks behind the counter and finds Howie's body.

He comes back to me just as Renny reaches my side. Carefully, I transfer Thea into his arms.

"Can she go?" I ask Sheriff Morales.

"Yes." He places a hand on Renny's shoulder. "I'll need to talk to her later."

Renny nods, sweeps Thea into his arms, and carries her across the street to where they rent a small apartment not far from the café.

Rebel walks into the café, and his face pales as he sees Howie's body. "Jesus."

"All right, everyone out," Carlos orders. "I don't want anyone contaminating the crime scene."

His deputies rush in, setting up a perimeter around the café. The youngest one, a fresh-faced kid barely out of high school, takes one look at Howie's remains and dashes outside, retching violently. I sympathize with him. The sight of Howie's blood pooling around his shattered skull will haunt me for a long time.

"Dammit." Carlos pinches the bridge of his nose. "This is bad, Dane. Really. Fucking. Bad."

"Tell me something I don't know." The memory of Howie's smiling face flashes through my mind, quickly followed by the image of his blood-soaked body on the floor. "He didn't deserve this."

Carlos' jaw tightens as he studies the chaotic scene one last time before gesturing for me to follow him. We stride through the shattered glass on the sidewalk, and he leads me back to the sheriff's station.

"You don't want your car?"

"No, it can stay where it is. I was on my way out to see the mayor at his house when the call came in." He turns to his deputies. "Stay here. If anyone asks, tell them nothing."

The sheriff's station is only a short distance from the café. Carlos leads me inside, through the bullpen, and into his office, where he slams the door shut behind us. A sea of papers and files litter the floor as he sweeps them off his desk in a rage.

"Goddammit, Dane!" Carlos bellows, losing his cool. "You had to go and bring this shitstorm to my town? To Howie?"

"Hey, don't pin this on me," I shoot back, my anger rising. "We don't shit where we eat, you know this. This isn't my fault."

"Fuck, I know," Carlos concedes, running a hand through his hair. "But Howie... he was just an innocent kid caught in the crossfire."

"Tell me about it." The image of Howie's lifeless body still burns in my mind, fueling the rage that simmers just beneath the surface. "He was good people, Carlos. He didn't deserve to die like that."

"None of us do." He sighs heavily, leaning against his desk. "But sometimes life doesn't give a fuck about what we deserve."

"Yeah."

None of us are angels—not me, not Carlos, and certainly not the rest of the MC. But it does not mean we deserve to be gunned down in cold blood.

"Look," Carlos' voice softens. "I know you're hurting, Dane. And I know you want revenge, but I need you to let me handle this. I don't need a damn gang war erupting in my town."

"It's my town too," I grumble, knowing deep down he is right. The last thing I want is for more innocent people to get caught in the crossfire. "But if your investigation doesn't turn up anything..."

"Then you can do what you have to do," he finishes, holding my gaze for a moment longer before turning away. "Now get out of here. And for fuck's sake, stay out of trouble."

"Can't make any promises," I reply with a bitter smirk, walking outside.

If it comes down to it, nothing will stand between avenging Howie's death and me, not even the law itself.

My cell phone buzzes in my pocket. "Talk to me."

"Prez," Jonas says, his voice tense. "We got them... the bastards responsible for the drive-by. They were sent by Tarso Lombardi."

Lombardi, the slimy fucker who thought he could take a shot at me. I clench my fists, trying to control my rage. "Good work, Jonas. Take them to The Barn."

"Understood." He hangs up, and I know he will take care of things from here.

"Everything all right?" Carlos asks as he joins me on the sidewalk.

"Handled," I reply, not wanting to give him any more details than necessary. "You need anything else from me?"

Carlos eyes me carefully, but instead of pressing me for information, he says, "Don't leave town."

"Got it." I nod, relieved he didn't push the issue.

As much as I respect Carlos, there are some things that need to be taken care of within the club without involving law enforcement.

As I walk away from the sheriff's station, I cannot help but think about the consequences of what I have set in motion. By ordering Jonas to deal with Lombardi's men, I know I am crossing a line that could put the MC and the town in even greater danger. But when it comes down to it, I have a responsibility to protect my own, and I am not about to let anyone threaten us without facing the consequences.

But I will be damned if I let any asshole take away what is mine without a fight.

I hit the button to dial Sal's number and wait for him to answer.

"Dane?"

"Sal, we have a problem. Lombardi's men tried to take me out. There will be retaliation for this shit."

"Jesus Christ," Sal replies. "You okay?"

"Fine, but Howie from Betty's didn't make it," I tell him, my voice thick with anger and grief. "We're going to war."

"Understood," Sal responds. "We'll be ready."

"Good. I'll keep you updated, and Sal, be careful." I hang up and try to keep my emotions in check. Right now, there is something else I need to do— break the news to Kat.

Six of my men follow me home, my mind racing with thoughts of how to tell her. She's been through so much already, and Howie's death will hit her hard. But she deserves to know the truth from me before it spreads through town.

"Hey, babe," I call out as I walk through the door, my voice strained. "We need to talk."

Kat looks up from where she sits on the couch, her eyes widening with concern when she sees the grim expression on my face. "What's wrong?" she asks, her voice barely above a whisper.

I take a deep breath. "Howie's dead, Kat." The words hit me like a punch to the gut. "Someone tried to take me out today, and he got caught in the crossfire."

Her green eyes fill with tears as she stares at me, heartbreak etched across her face. "No," she whispers, shaking her head in disbelief. "Howie... he was like family to us."

I nod, my throat tight with emotion. "I know, darlin'. I'm so sorry."

"Are you okay?" Her voice cracks. "You weren't hurt, were you?"

Shaking my head, I sit next to her on the couch

and pull her onto my lap. "No. They missed."

Kat lets out a shaky breath and wraps her arms around my neck. We stay like that, wrapped in each other's arms, until Jesse comes running into the room.

"Are you two having alone time?" he asks.

Kat laughs and looks at him. "No, son. Daddy's just had a bad day. He needs a hug."

Kat gets off my lap, and Jesse climbs on.

"Are you sad, Daddy?"

Holding him close, I shake my head. "No, Jesse. How could I be when I have you, your sister, and your brothers."

"What about Mom?"

Winking at Kat, I say, "Ahh, yes, and your mom."

CHAPTER
18

DANE

The stench of oil and sweat hangs heavy in the air as I stand beside Kade, my sergeant-at-arms, in the dimly lit garage. The Chicago chapter of the Savage Angels MC have gathered for an emergency Church meeting to discuss the shitstorm that is about to rain down on us. The Lombardi family has crossed a fucking line, trying to kill me, and I will be damned if we do not hit them back *hard.*

"All right, brothers, let's get this started," I bark, slamming my fist on the makeshift table before us. "As most of you know, the Lombardis tried to take me out."

Anger ripples through the group, the tension in the room crackling like a live wire.

"Enough!" I roar, silencing the room. "We aren't

going sit around and wait for them to strike again. We're going to hit them hard." The conviction in my voice echoes off the walls, reverberating with the rumble of bikes outside.

"Yo, Dane," Onyx speaks up, his dark eyes lock onto me, demanding my attention. "No disrespect, Prez, but are we gonna exact some *real* revenge on these assholes or just sit on our bikes all day lookin' mean?"

Rage flares inside of me.

The nerve of this guy.

But he is right.

This isn't a time for idle threats. I need to show my brothers we were taking this fight seriously.

"Listen up! I know the last time we geared up for war, we were asked to back down. We wanted to prevent bloodshed on both sides." My eyes lock onto each member of the Chicago chapter as I continue, "But this time, no one is going to stand in our way. We're taking the Lombardis down, and we won't stop until they pay for what they've done."

My brothers nod their silent agreement, knowing full well this isn't only about me—it is about the Savage Angels MC and everything we stand for.

The heavy door swings open, revealing Sal. The room goes deadly quiet, the tension thick enough to cut with a knife.

"Sal," I say, extending my hand and pulling him

into a tight bro-hug. "Glad you could make it."

"Anything for family," he replies, his dark eyes meeting mine. Sal might be part of the Italian mob, but he is a brother to me, and I will be damned if anyone disrespects him.

"Listen up!" I bark, turning back to the club. "This here is Salvatore Agostino, brother to me and a friend to the MC. We show him respect, got it?" A few men exchange uneasy glances, not accustomed to having someone from the mafia in our midst, let alone on sacred ground. However, none dare oppose me considering I am the president of the mother chapter.

"Thank you, Dane." Sal addresses the room, "I come here to offer my help. We share a common enemy, and there's nothing more important than honor."

I can see the uncertainty in my brothers' eyes, but I trust Sal, and if he is willing to lend a hand, we would be fools not to accept it.

"Can I speak with you in private, Dane?" Sal asks.

"Sure," I reply, leading him out of the crowded room and into the cool night air.

"I know where Tarso Lombardi is hiding. I want to help you take him down." His eyes bore into mine, letting me know he meant every damn word.

I take a deep breath, letting the chill of the night air fill my lungs before I speak, "I appreciate that, Sal. Really, I do. But this is something the Savage

Angels must handle on their own. We need to show the Lombardi fucks we aren't playing games."

Sal seems to think for a moment, his eyes narrowing as he considers something. Then, he looks back at me with resolve in his gaze. "All right, Dane. I have another idea. What if I call a meeting with the families? You know, to draw Tarso Lombardi out into the open. I have a warehouse down by the docks... private and secluded. The Savage Angels can wait inside for him."

I weigh his words, my mind racing through the possibilities. We have been through a lot together, him and the MC.

But this is different.

This is war.

"Tomorrow night," I finally say. Decision made. "We'll do it tomorrow night."

Sal nods. "I'll set it up. We're going to take that son of a bitch down once and for all."

"Let's hope so." I turn on my heel and head back into the clubhouse.

The room is buzzing, my brothers eager for action. They can feel it in the air, the electricity of what is about to go down. I stand in front of them, letting my eyes roam over every one of them— these men who've become my comrades, who I'll fight and die for without a second thought.

"Listen up!" The chatter comes to a halt. "We've got a plan. Sal's going to call a meeting with the families tomorrow night. Tarso Lombardi will be there, and we're going to be waiting for him."

A murmur of approval ripples through the room, and I see the fire in their eyes—that same hunger for vengeance that burns inside me.

"Tomorrow night, we show these Lombardi fucks what happens when you mess with the Savage Angels MC."

A roar erupts from my brothers, the sound shaking the walls and making my heart pound hard.

The warehouse is a grimy, forgotten place—the kind of spot where the sun does not shine and hope goes to die. Cobwebs hang thick in the corners and the air reeks of mold and decay. This is our battleground—the stage for the showdown that will end the feud between us and the Lombardi scum.

I stand with my brothers, our guns drawn and ready. Salvatore Agostino and Tony are by my side, their eyes as cold and unyielding as steel. Heavy plastic sheets line the floor, a cruel reminder of the bloodshed that is about to unfold.

One by one, the Italian families file into the

warehouse, their uneasy expressions telling me all I need to know. They are not comfortable here, surrounded by bikers and bracing for violence. But they know better than to cross the Savage Angels or the Agostinos.

"Keep it cool, boys," I whisper, my gaze never leaving the entrance. "We'll get our shot soon enough."

Kiyoko is the last to enter the room, her delicate frame belying the iron will beneath. She strides to me, her eyes locking onto mine without a trace of fear. Her gloved hand extends, and I take it firmly, respect passing between us in that single moment.

"Good luck, Dane," she murmurs, her voice soft but steely. "Make them pay."

"Count on it, darlin'," I reply, giving her a nod before turning back to the door.

Tarso Lombardi enters the warehouse last, his eyes widening as he takes in the scene laid out before him. My blood boils merely at the sight of him, the man responsible for so much pain and suffering. His gaze drifts over the Savage Angels who flank the walls, and I see the realization dawning in his eyes—he has walked into a trap.

But pride is a hell of a thing, and it will not let Tarso back down. With a sneer and a swagger that speaks of a false sense of security, he marches forward into the warehouse, ready to face whatever fate has in store for him.

"Let's get this over with," he spits, his eyes darting between Salvatore and me.

My grip tightens on my gun, and my heart pounds heavily as I prepare for the storm that is about to break loose.

"Your time's up, Lombardi," I growl, my voice low and dangerous. "You're going to pay for everything you've done."

"Bring it, Reynolds," he shoots back, his arrogant smirk only fueling my rage. "I ain't afraid of you or your pathetic little gang of misfits."

"Well, that's your first mistake," I state.

Tarso's sneer turns contemptuous as he surveys the Savage Angels, his eyes lingering on me with disgust. "You really thought you could take me down, Reynolds?" he scoffs. "You're nothin' but a bunch of lowlife bikers playin' at bein' tough."

His gaze shifts to Salvatore, and the venom in his voice increases tenfold. "And you, Sal. You had to go and ally yourself with these pieces of trash? Betray your own kind?"

Salvatore steps forward, his posture calm but his eyes burning with anger.

He glances around the room, addressing the other Italian family heads gathered for this meeting. "Does anyone else here have a problem with the Agostino Crime Family working alongside the Savage Angels MC?"

The tension in the room is palpable, but no one

speaks up. They know better than to cross Sal. Even Tarso, though he will not back down completely, stays silent.

"Didn't think so," Salvatore says coolly, holding Tarso's glare.

Tarso spits on the ground at Sal's feet, a clear sign of disrespect. I can feel the tension in the air—the point of no return. It is time to put an end to this, once and for all.

"Big mistake, Lombardi," I growl, my hand flexing on my gun. It will not be long now before everything comes to a head, and I am ready to see this through to the bitter end.

As I stand there, the suspense thicker than smoke in the air, one of Tarso's men makes his move. The sound of a gunshot slices through the silence like a razor, and before I know it, the bullet tears across my cheek, the sting sharp as hell.

"Fuck!" I spit, but even as I do, Kade is already on it. He steps forward, gun raised, and puts a bullet straight through the dumb fuck's head who took the shot at me. The man crumples to the floor like a sack of bones, blood pooling around him. I am grateful to Kade for his quick reflexes, but the gratitude is quickly swallowed by rage, heating my blood like molten lava.

The metallic taste of blood fills my mouth as it trickles down from the gash on my cheek. It mingles with the fury boiling inside me, and I lock my eyes on Tarso, stalking toward him with deadly intent.

Holstering my gun, my lips curl back in a snarl as I say, "You piece of shit." All concerns about caring if anyone else hears, vanish. "You're going to pay for this."

Tarso scrambles for his gun, but I am quicker. My hand shoots out, drawing my blade from its sheath. In one fluid motion, I plunge it deep into his chest, feeling it bite through flesh, muscle, and bone. His eyes widen, disbelief and shock written all over his face as he stares down at the steel buried in him.

"Wha... what have you done?" he gasps, straining to breathe, clinging to the last shreds of life.

"Finishing what you started, Tarso." I hold his gaze steady as the light in his eyes begins to flicker and fade.

I watch as the realization that death is coming for him settles in, and his once-cocky expression crumbles into desperation. His mouth opens, but no sound comes out, only a wet gurgle as blood bubbles up in his throat.

"See you in hell, Lombardi," I whisper, my voice colder than ice, before yanking the knife free from his chest. Tarso's body hits the floor with a heavy thud, lifeless and defeated.

Wiping the blade on Tarso's shirt, I cannot help but feel a sense of satisfaction. This piece of shit has tried to take me down, but he failed, and now he is the one lying dead at my feet.

Kathleen Kelly

"Anyone else want to fuck with the Savage Angels?" I bellow, my voice echoing through the warehouse. Silence answers me, and I know the message has been sent loud and clear—nobody messes with Dane Reynolds or his brothers without paying the ultimate price.

With blood dripping down my cheek, I turn to face the room once more. Heads of families and gang members alike all stare at the bloody aftermath, but none will dare challenge the Savage Angels now.

"Anyone else got a problem with our alliance?" Salvatore calmly asks, his gaze sweeping across the tense faces. "Good," he says when no one speaks up. "Now, let's get on with business."

I stand beside Salvatore, the Agostino family, and the Savage Angels surrounding us, united and stronger for what we have been through. We might come from different worlds, the mafia and the MC, but we understand each other in ways that matter most—love, loyalty, family, and taking care of those who threaten it.

CHAPTER 19

DANE

Pulling up to the house I built, hoping one day it would become a home, I think back to the first day I met Kat. It wasn't until she entered its doorway that it became a home. These walls house my everything I hold dear, the ones I will always protect.

The roar of my bike's engine dies down as I park in front of our home, the place where life makes most sense.

"Mom! Dad's here!" I hear Jesse shout from inside, and the door bursts open as he and Kristen rush out with Kat close behind.

"Hey, Daddy!" they yell in unison, launching themselves at me.

My arms wrap around them instinctively,

holding on tight. "Hey yourself," I choke out, feeling something catch in my throat.

I look up at Kat, her green eyes shining with relief and love. She is a sight for sore eyes, and damn, do I need that right now.

"Welcome home, babe." Her hand reaches up to touch my face gently near the butterfly plasters.

I lean into her touch, needing the comfort only she can provide. But the moment is short-lived as the kids squirm in my arms, eager for attention.

"All right, all right." I laugh, ruffling their hair before setting them down. "Let's go inside."

Stepping through the door, the familiar surroundings and the scent of Kat's perfume mixed with the smell of dinner on the stove is overwhelming. My body aches, and the exhaustion seems to seep into my bones, but it is not only physical. The emotional toll of the past few weeks and the danger we have faced has consumed me, and the fear for my family's safety gnaws at my insides like a hungry beast.

"Can I get you anything?" Kat asks, noticing my weariness.

All I want is to collapse into her arms, but I know the kids need me too.

"Maybe just a few minutes to sit down and breathe," I reply, rubbing the back of my neck. "Then we can all catch up."

"Sounds good." She gives me a soft smile before

turning to the kids. "Why don't you guys go wash up for dinner?"

"Okay, Mom," they yell, scattering in different directions like only kids can.

I sink into our worn leather couch, every muscle in my body screaming for rest as Kat settles next to me. I do not have to say anything. She can read the exhaustion on my face as plain as day.

"Rough ride?" she asks, her voice full of concern as she stares at my cheek.

"Yeah," I admit, letting out a deep breath. "But I'm home now, and that's all that matters."

"Hey," Kat whispers, drawing me out of my thoughts as she cups my face lightly in her hands, her vivid green eyes searching mine. "You're home, Dane." She traces a finger along the wound on my cheek. "Chicks dig scars, you know," she teases, a grin tugging at her lips. "Makes you look even more badass."

"Is that so?" I quirk an eyebrow, my lips turning up in a small smile.

"Absolutely." She winks, placing a tender kiss on the plasters.

It is moments like these that remind me why I fight so hard and push myself to my limits for my family and club. They are worth every ounce of pain and struggle.

"Kat, things have been rough lately. But I swear to you, no harm will come to you, our kids, or the

MC as long as I'm breathing."

Her eyes shine with love and admiration. "I know, Dane. You've always been our rock. But honey, you don't have to do it alone. We're all in this together."

The sound of laughter fills our home, a welcome backdrop to the chaos that has become all too familiar lately. Kat and I sit on the floor, surrounded by our kids, while they tell me all about their brothers, Blaze and Gunner, who are asleep upstairs.

A bell sounds from the kitchen, and Kat stands. "Who's going to help me serve dinner?"

"I'll set the table," says Jesse as he runs for the kitchen with Kat following him

"Sucker." Kristen laughs as she watches her twin disappear.

"That's not nice, young lady."

The smile almost falls from her face, and she says, "Sorry, Dad."

"Go on in and help."

She does as she's told but drags her feet. I know Kristen loves her brother, but even from an early age, she has been able to twist him around her little finger.

Jesse is putting cutlery on the table for us, and when I scowl at Kristen, she begins putting the plates down. Kat hands me a large bowl of rice which I place in the center of the table, and she carries over a chicken curry dish.

As a one, we sit down, Kat ladles out the rice, and I put the chicken on everyone's plate.

This is what home is to me.

All of us together, enjoying a meal and each other's company.

Later that night, after tucking the kids into bed, I pull Kat close, savoring the warmth of her body pressed against mine. Her light brown hair, streaked with sun-kissed blonde, cascades over her shoulders, and I brush it back gently, revealing the curve of her neck.

"Tonight reminds me how much we mean to each other." My lips graze her earlobe. "I'll never take that for granted."

"Neither will I." Her fingers play with the hem of my shirt, then with a wicked grin, she adds, "Now let's make up for lost time."

Our mouths meet in a hungry kiss, tongues tangling as we tear off each other's clothes. The world around us ceases to exist as we fall onto the bed, our bodies a tangle of skin, muscles, and heat as we explore each other's forms with urgent and desperate touches. My hands roam over Kat's curves, desperate for more skin-to-skin contact. Every touch ignites sparks of pleasure as her body melds with mine.

"God, Dane." Kat moans, her nails digging into my back. "I missed you so much."

"Never gonna let you go again," I growl, my voice thick with desire.

"I need you."

Smiling, I give a slight shake of my head. "Not until you've had a good time."

Kat places a hand on my face. "Silly man. I want you inside me. I want you to bury yourself in me and make me yours."

"You already are."

Kat smiles. "And I always will be."

Her hand moves to my cock, and she guides me between her legs. Her slick, tight pussy takes every inch of me as she holds my gaze.

"I love you." I gasp as I pull out and thrust back in.

"Not as much as I love you."

And as we crest the waves of pleasure together, our hearts beating in unison, I know that no matter what trials lay ahead, we will face them together.

The sun creeps up over the horizon, casting warm hues of orange and pink across the sky. I stand on the back porch of our home in Tourmaline, a steaming cup of coffee in hand, as Kat wraps her arms around me from behind. Her touch is a reminder of the strength we have found in each other despite all the challenges we have faced.

"Looks like it's going to be a beautiful day." Kat rests her chin on my back.

"Sure is, darlin'," I reply, sipping my coffee. "Feels good to be home."

"Time for us to enjoy some peace." The sound of many Harleys fills the air as she says the words, her voice filled with hope. "Here they come. I'm going to make another pot of coffee." Kat goes up on her tiptoes and kisses me. "I've also defrosted a bunch of steaks. You're on barbecue detail."

"You arranged this?"

"Yeah, I figured you would want to see your brothers, but I want to keep you home with me, so I invited the hoards here."

Laughing, I say, "I got lucky the day you agreed to marry me."

"Yes, apart from me getting shot on our wedding

day, yeah, we both got lucky."

The first people to make it through the house are Kade and Destiny.

"Prez," he says by way of a greeting and holds up a six-pack of beer. "Thanks for the invite."

We clasp hands, and I pull him in for a slap on his back. "You know damn well it wasn't me, but thanks for the beer."

Bear, with Shaz close behind him, walks out and looks around. "Want me to light up the barbecue?"

"Yeah, brother, appreciate it."

Someone turns on the music, and it echoes through the house.

"Hey, Prez!" one of the guys calls out, raising a coffee cup in a salute. "Glad to have you back!"

"Thanks, brother," I reply, clinking my cup against his. "I'm happy everyone's safe and sound."

As the morning turns into the afternoon, Kat and I sit together on a bench, watching the festivities unfold. She leans into me, her body radiating warmth as I wrap an arm around her shoulders.

"Look at them, Dane," she whispers, nodding toward our children. "They're happy. Safe. That's all that matters." Her green eyes search mine. "Promise me we'll never let anything come between us."

"I promise, Kat," I vow, my voice unwavering. "From this moment on, it's you and me against the world."

Kat laughs, and I arch an eyebrow at her. "Babe, that's what Truth says to Rosie. You've been hanging out with my bandmates far too much."

Laughing, I nod. "How about love and loyalty always?"

"Better." Kat kisses me, then stands and walks inside the house.

The atmosphere shifts from boisterous to serene as the day drags on. The MC members gather around a fire, sharing stories of past adventures and offering words of gratitude.

"Here's to the future," I toast, raising my beer bottle high. "To the Savage Angels, to family, and to the life we've built together."

"May it always be wild, beautiful, and free," Kat adds, her eyes shining.

As we stand there, united by love and loyalty, I know we will conquer every challenge that threatens to tear us apart. Together, we are unstoppable. And no matter what lies ahead, we will face it as one with courage, passion, and the unbreakable bonds of the Savage Angels MC.

Our confrontation with the Lombardis may have tarnished our wings, but one thing holds true—we value love and loyalty above all else.

EPILOGUE

JESSE REYNOLDS
Patched-in Member, the Savage Angels MC
Fifteen Years Later

The streets of Maplewood are quiet at two o'clock in the morning as I weave through the seedy part of town. Winter is coming. I can feel the chill in the air as I stick to the shadows. The person I'm looking for should be in the run-down white house up ahead.

The stench of piss and stale alcohol cling to the air as I stand outside the rundown shithole. I kick open the worn door, stepping into the dimly lit room. The floorboards creak beneath my boots, and dirty, cracked walls close in around me, but I do not give a fuck. I am here for one reason and one reason only.

"Who the fuck are you?" the greasy man on the couch asks, eyeing me up and down. He looks like he hasn't showered in weeks, his skin glistening with filth.

"Savage Angels don't do drugs anymore."

The man's eyes widen in surprise, but he quickly regains his composure, laughing cynically. "Ha! That ain't what the princess told me, kid," he sneers. "Been dealin' with your crew for months now."

My blood boils at the mention of my twin sister. Kristen is spiraling out of control, and this bastard is feeding her habits. The fucker has no idea who I am or who he is messing with.

"Listen up, asshole," I snarl. "You've been misinformed. You're done peddling your shit to my people. You hear me?"

"Or what, pretty boy?" he mocks me, leaning back against the torn-up sofa. "You gonna send your daddy after me?"

Shit, he *does* know who I am.

"Shut your fucking mouth," I seethe, trying to keep my anger in check. Losing control right now is not an option.

"Or what?" he repeats, his laughter turning into a sinister grin. "You ain't got the balls to do shit."

"Keep pushing me," I warn, my voice low and dangerous. "See what happens."

"Jesse? What the fuck are you doing here?"

Kristen slurs as she stumbles into the room. Her eyes are glassy and unfocused, her movements sluggish. She is clearly high as a kite.

"Kristen," I grit out, my heart clenching at the sight of her in such a state. "Get out of here."

"Relax, Jesse," she drawls, swaying slightly on her feet. "I'm only here for my shit." She tosses a bag to the dealer, who smirks triumphantly.

"See, pretty boy? Your princess knows who she's dealing with," he taunts as he stands and hands Kristen a larger bag filled with bricks of heroin.

"Give me that," I demand, reaching for the bag in Kristen's hand, but she pulls away, her eyes narrowing in defiance.

"Back off, Jesse," she hisses. "You don't control me."

"Like hell I don't," I retort, my patience wearing thin.

I am tired of cleaning up her messes and watching her destroy herself. But deep down, I know I will never be able to turn my back on her, not when she needs me most.

"Fine, do what the fuck you want," I snap, stepping back. "But remember, Kristen, I ain't always gonna be around to save your ass."

"Who says I need saving?" She clutches the bag of heroin to her chest like it is a lifeline. "Get out of here, Jesse. Go play hero somewhere else."

"Kristen, please," I plead, my anger giving way to

desperation. "This shit's going to get you killed. Using and dealing are a dangerous mix. Don't do this to yourself. Don't do this to us."

"Us?" she scoffs, her voice dripping with disdain. "There is no 'us,' Jesse. You chose your precious club over me a long time ago."

"Fuck that!" My frustration boils over once more. "I've been trying to protect you, Kristen. But you keep running back to this poison like it's your goddamn salvation!"

"Maybe it is," she whispers, tears brimming in her unfocused eyes. "Maybe it's the only thing keeping me alive."

"Your life is worth more than this," I say softly, my heart breaking for her. "You don't have to live like this, sis."

"Leave me alone, Jesse."

My heart pounds in my chest, and my hands shake with fury as I pull out my gun. Without a second thought, I shove the barrel of the weapon into the man's mouth, forcing him backward until his head bounces off a wall.

"Jesse, stop!" Kristen screams, her voice frantic and desperate.

"Shut up, Kristen," I growl, my eyes locked on the drug dealer's terrified gaze. "She's cut off," I warn him, pushing the gun further into his mouth. "You don't supply my sister with your shit anymore, or I will find you and kill you." Fear fills the air as he whimpers. "Got it?"

He nods as best he can, and I remove the gun from his mouth, leaving him coughing and gasping for breath.

Grabbing Kristen by the hand, I lead her back through the rundown house, her protests falling on deaf ears.

"Let go of me, Jesse!" she yells, trying to wrestle herself free from my grip. "I can take care of myself!"

"Like hell you can," I shoot back, my anger fueled by the knowledge that she is slipping further away from me every day. "You're coming with me whether you like it or not."

"Fuck you!"

We reach my bike, and I force her onto the back before climbing on and revving the engine. As we speed through the streets of Maplewood, I think about how far we've come and how much farther apart we seem to be drifting.

The wind whips at my face, clearing my head as I focus on getting us back to Tourmaline. Despite everything, I still love my sister, and I will do whatever it takes to save her from herself, even if that means putting my own life on the line.

"Jesse," Kristen whispers, her voice barely audible over the bike's roar. "I'm sorry."

"Don't apologize to me," I tell her, my voice tight with emotion. "Just promise me you'll try to get better for both our sakes."

"I'll try." Her arms tighten around my waist as we leave Maplewood behind and speed toward Tourmaline, our home.

The siren blares, cutting through the wind as we speed along the outskirts of Tourmaline. I glance over my shoulder at the familiar face of Sheriff Carlos Morales behind the wheel of his cruiser.

Shit.

"Don't pull over," Kristen groans against my back. "He's gonna arrest us."

"Shut up," I snap as I reluctantly ease off the throttle and guide the bike to a stop on the side of the road.

Carlos pulls up alongside us, his steely eyes scanning us with disappointment. "Jesse, what the hell are you doing? Do you know how fast you were going?" he demands to know, his voice gruff. He stares at Kristen for a moment before shaking his head. "Dammit, girl. You're high. Get in the back of my car."

Kristen hesitates, her eyes flicking to me in panic. I nod tersely, signaling her to obey. As she climbs unsteadily into the cruiser, Carlos rounds on me.

"Want to tell me what's going on?" he asks, crossing his arms and studying me intently. But I will never rat out my sister, even if it means getting myself into deeper shit.

"Nothing," I reply, keeping my tone level. "Just taking her for a ride."

"Like hell." Carlos eyes me suspiciously. He reaches for the saddlebag on my bike and yanks it open, revealing the open bag with the bricks of heroin. His expression darkens. "You got some explaining to do, Jesse."

"Put your hands on the bike," he orders, his voice cold.

I comply, swallowing hard as he handcuffs me and leads me to the back of the cruiser. My heart races as I try to work out how I managed to get us into this mess.

As Carlos drives toward the sheriff's station, I cast a glance at Kristen. She's staring blankly out the window, her gaze is distant and vacant. The sight of her like this almost breaks me, but I have to stay strong.

"Carlos," I say, my voice catching in my throat. "Please, just let her go. This ain't her fault."

"Can't do that, Jesse," he replies, his tone surprisingly gentle. "I've known you two since you were born, and it kills me to see what she's become.

But covering up for her won't help her get better."

"Then what will?" My frustration spills over. "She needs help, not a damn jail cell."

"First thing's first," he says, his gaze meeting mine in the mirror. "We need to call your dad."

A cold wave of dread washes over me at the mention of my father.

Carlos is right!

Things are about to get a whole lot worse.

The heavy metal door of the sheriff's station creaks open, casting a shadow across the cold linoleum floor. My heart pounds in my chest as I watch my father stride in, his tall frame and broad shoulders filling the doorway. The years have only made him more formidable. His dark hair is peppered with gray, but his icy-blue eyes still burn with intensity.

"Carlos," he rumbles.

"Appreciate you coming down, Dane." They have known each other for as long as I can remember, and although I wouldn't say they are best friends, they have a healthy respect for each other. "We've got a problem."

Dad tilts his head to the side and looks at me

through the jail cell's bars. Carlos walks closer to me down the narrow hallway of the holding cells. I can feel the cold metal of the handcuffs biting into my wrists when I stand, trying to appear strong despite the fear gnawing at my insides.

Dad's gaze shifts between Kristen's disheveled state and my tense expression before settling on the bag Carlos holds out to him.

"Found this on Jesse's bike," Carlos explains, opening the bag to reveal the bricks of heroin inside. "He claims it isn't Kristen's fault."

I brace myself for the storm that is about to hit, knowing full well that my father will never tolerate drugs in his club. As he stares at the bag's contents, his face morphs into a mask of pure fury.

"Jesse!" he bellows, his anger echoing off the walls. "What the fuck is this?"

"Look, Dad, I can explain—" I begin, but he cuts me off with a glare that chills me to my core.

"Explain? You better have a *damn good* explanation, boy. The Savage Angels don't run drugs anymore. We're clean."

Not wanting to get my sister in trouble, I say nothing.

"Please, Dad," Kristen whispers, her voice barely audible. "It's not Jesse—"

"Silence!" he roars, causing her to flinch. "You've brought shame on the club, Jesse. You're damn lucky Carlos is willing to give you a second chance."

My stomach churns, knowing I have let my father down—the one man who's always been there for me. It is all too clear I have no choice but to face the consequences of my actions, even if it means losing everything I hold dear.

Carlos sighs heavily as he looks at the bag of heroin. "I'll destroy this, Dane," his voice is stern yet tired. "No charges for Jesse or Kristen, but you need to get your house in order."

"Thank you, Carlos. Appreciate it," Dad replies, his expression a mix of gratitude and frustration. He turns to Kristen, guiding her out of the cell with a firm hand. "Let's go, princess."

As the sound of their footsteps echoes down the hallway, I am left alone with Carlos. The sheriff shakes his head and leans against the wall, arms crossed over his chest.

"Jesse..." he says, meeting my eyes with a hard stare. "It's about time you let Kristen pay the price for her mistakes instead of covering for her."

The weight of his words settles on me like a lead blanket, but I remain silent, unable to form a response that would make any difference.

When Dad returns, his eyes bore into me with an intensity that makes me feel small. A rare occurrence for someone who's grown up under the watchful gaze of the Savage Angels' president.

"Go to the clubhouse," he orders, his voice tight with restrained anger. "I'm takin' Kristen home."

"All right, Dad." I rise from the cold bench, and Carlos undoes my handcuffs, then I head for the exit.

The walk back to the compound takes me less than ten minutes.

I can't shake the feeling that things are about to change, and not for the better.

Taking the steps two at a time, I enter the clubhouse.

Rebel is sitting alone at a table, and he smiles at me. "Jesse, what brings you out so early?"

"Reb, can you give me a lift back to my bike? The sheriff picked me up for speeding, and it's on the outskirts of town."

Rebel laughs. "Did he give you a ticket? Your old man is going to be pissed."

"You have no idea."

Rebel gives me a strange look but asks me nothing further as we walk out to his bike.

The ride back to my Harley is thankfully uneventful. Climbing off Rebel's bike, I mount mine, and we head back to the clubhouse.

Carlos' words are swirling around in my head.

Am I doing Kristen any favors by constantly shielding her from the consequences of her actions? Or am I simply making everything worse?

The truth hits me like a punch to the gut—I have failed Kristen and the club. And now, it is time to face whatever punishment my father has in store for me.

When we pull up at the clubhouse, Rebel's cell phone chimes. He pulls it out of his pocket and frowns. "What have you done?"

I shrug. "Why?"

Rebel scowls at me. "Your dad wants you to wait in your room until you are called."

Fuck.

"He's called a meeting?"

Rebel nods.

Fuck me, I've really screwed up this time. With a curt nod, I walk through the clubhouse and to my room. Laying on the bed, I stare up at the ceiling. Should I tell Dad the drugs were Kristen's and not mine? Should I tell him I found out she's been dealing and using? I'm not sure she could stand Dad's wrath or disappointment.

After an hour of doing nothing, a knock sounds on my door, and Jonas opens it. "You're wanted in the chapel."

From the expression on his face, this isn't good. I stand and follow him through the clubhouse, which is eerily quiet.

The heavy chapel door creaks open, and I feel every eye in the room on me as I step inside. The room feels thick with tension, a storm brewing beneath the surface. I keep my hands at my sides, so I appear unfazed, even though I know whatever is coming will not be easy to swallow.

"Jesse," Dad's voice is cold and distant. I have never seen him this angry at me. "Sit," he orders, pointing to an empty chair among the other Savage Angels gathered around the table. As I take my place, the familiar faces of my brothers stare back at me, their expressions a mix of pity and disappointment.

It is like a knife to the heart, but I know I deserve it.

Dad wastes no time getting to the point. "You've put the club at risk, Jesse. We don't deal drugs anymore, and you know it. But because of you, we're now tied to that filth again, and worst of all, you brought that shit here to our home."

"Sorry, Dad." I stare at the wooden tabletop, unable to look my father in the eyes. "The deal wasn't supposed to go down the way it did. I swear."

"Enough," he snaps, silencing any further excuses I might have offered. "Your actions have consequences, and you need to learn that the hard way…" He pauses, inhaling deeply before delivering the blow which will change everything. "You're banished to Las Vegas."

My breath catches in my throat as his words hit me full force.

Banished.

To fucking Las Vegas.

My father is disowning me.

Looking up at him, I search his face for any hint of mercy, but in his eyes, I find nothing but disappointment.

"Wha... Dad, I... you can't be serious," I stammer, my voice barely a whisper.

"Dead fucking serious, Jesse." His voice is like steel, and it cuts me like a knife. "You'll be riding out tomorrow morning."

A thousand emotions threaten to explode inside me, but I swallow them, knowing that arguing will only make things worse. My brothers watch in silence as I struggle to come to terms with my new reality.

I have always dreamed of one day taking over the Tourmaline chapter, earning my father's respect and making him proud. Now, it is all slipping through my fingers, leaving me grasping at the ashes of a future that will never be mine.

"Understood," I choke out, nodding my head in submission. It is the only word I can manage, but it speaks volumes about the pain and regret that consumes me.

"Good." Dad turns away from me as if I am already gone. "Now get out of my sight."

With a heavy heart, I push back from the table and leave the chapel, feeling the weight of my father's disappointment settle on my shoulders like a crushing burden. As I walk away, I wonder what lies ahead for me in Las Vegas and whether I will ever find my way back home.

The next morning, I'm packing my gear when Bear walks in. "Jesse, you sure you're okay with this?"

"Does it fucking matter?" I snap, my anger flaring. "Ain't like I got a choice."

"Easy, man," Jonas says from behind Bear. "We're all worried about you, but don't take it out on us."

"Sorry." I run a hand through my hair as I attempt to regain control of my emotions.

They are only trying to help, but I can't shake the feeling that everything I have worked for is crumbling around me.

"Las Vegas ain't so bad," Rebel chimes in, trying to lighten the mood. "Maybe it'll be good for you, brother."

"Sure," I reply bitterly, my thoughts consumed by the betrayal I feel for my father.

Looking around my room, memories of growing up within these walls flood my mind. Every laugh, every fight, every moment spent dreaming of one day leading the Tourmaline chapter.

But now, those dreams are shattered, replaced by the uncertainty of a future I have not asked for and do not want. The weight of it all threatens to crush me, but I force myself to push it away, focusing instead on the need to prove myself to my father and my club. I will not let them see me break.

"Las Vegas, huh?" I mutter more to myself as the reality of it all starts to sink in. "Maybe I'll show them what a real Savage Angel can do."

The three men, who are all like fathers to me, escort me out of the clubhouse. With a renewed sense of purpose, I leave the compound behind, my mind set on proving that even though I have been banished from Tourmaline, I am still a force to be reckoned with.

And maybe, just maybe, I can find a way to earn back everything I have lost or...

... forge a new path in Las Vegas.

THE END

The Savage Angels will continue with
Jesse Reynolds in the
Las Vegas chapter in late 2024.

If you liked this story,
you can continue with
other books by Kathleen Kelly.

The MacKenny Brothers Series
An MC/Band of Brothers Romance
Spark Book 1
Spark of Vengeance Book 2
Spark of Hope Book 3
Spark of Deception Book 4
Spark of Time Book 5
Spark of Redemption Book 6
Spark of Passion Book 7

Tackling Romance Series
A Sports Romance
Tackling Love Book 1
Tackling Life Book 2

Standalones
Wraith
Fealty: A Wraith Novel
Cardinal: The Affinity Chronicles Book One
Crude Possession: Crude Souls MC

Savage Angels

Snake's Revenge: Gritty Devils MC

The Savage Angels MC Series
Motorcycle Club Romance
Savage Stalker Book 1
Savage Fire Book 2
Savage Town Book 3
Savage Lover Book 4
Savage Sacrifice Book 5
Savage Rebel (Novella) Book 6
Savage Lies Book 7
Savage Life Book 8
Savage Christmas (Novella) Book 9
Savage Release Book 10
Savage Heart Book 11
Savage Angels Book 12

Royal Bastards MC Jacksonville, FL

Creed Book 1
Reaper Book 2
Highway Book 3

CONNECT WITH ME ONLINE

Check these links for more books from
Author Kathleen Kelly

READER GROUP

Want access to fun, prizes and sneak peeks?
Join my Facebook Reader Group.
https://bit.ly/32X17pv

NEWSLETTER

Want to see what's next?
Sign up for my Newsletter.
https://www.subscribepage.com/kathleenkellyauthor

BOOKBUB

Connect with me on Bookbub.
https://www.bookbub.com/authors/kathleen-kelly

GOODREADS

Add my books to your TBR list
on my Goodreads profile.
http://bit.ly/1xsOGxk

AMAZON

Buy my books from my Amazon profile.
https://amzn.to/2JCUT6q

WEBSITE

https://kathleenkellyauthor.com/

TIKTOK

https://www.tiktok.com/@kathleenkellyauthor

TWITTER

https://twitter.com/kkellyauthor

INSTAGRAM

https://instagram.com/kathleenkellyauthor

EMAIL

kathleenkellyauthor@gmail.com

FACEBOOK

https://bit.ly/36jlaQV

ABOUT THE AUTHOR

Kathleen Kelly was born in Penrith, NSW, Australia. When she was four, her family moved to Brisbane, QLD, Australia. Although born in NSW, she considers herself a QUEENSLANDER!

She married her childhood sweetheart, and they live in Toowoomba.

Kathleen enjoys writing contemporary romance novels with a little bit of steam. She draws her inspiration from family, friends, and the people around her. She can often be found in cafes writing and observing the locals.

If you have any questions about her novels or would like to ask Kathleen a question, she can be contacted via e-mail:

kathleenkellyauthor@gmail.com

or she can be found on Facebook. She loves to be contacted by those who love her books.